Death By Chance

A Josiah Reynolds Mystery
Book Sixteen

Abigail Keam

Worker Bee Press

Book cover by Cricket Press.

Edited by Penny Baker.

Author's photograph by Peter Keam.

Special thanks to Melanie Murphy and Liz Hobson.

ISBN 978 1 953478 05 4
92721

Published in the USA by

Worker Bee Press
P.O. Box 485
Nicholasville, KY 40340

Books By Abigail Keam

Josiah Reynolds Mysteries
Death By A HoneyBee I
Death By Drowning II
Death By Bridle III
Death By Bourbon IV
Death By Lotto V
Death By Chocolate VI
Death By Haunting VII
Death By Derby VIII
Death By Design IX
Death By Malice X
Death By Drama XI
Death By Stalking XII
Death By Deceit XIII
Death By Magic XIV
Death By Shock XV
Death By Chance XVI

The Mona Moon Mystery Series
Murder Under A Blue Moon I
Murder Under A Blood Moon II
Murder Under A Bad Moon III
Murder Under A Silver Moon IV
Murder Under A Wolf Moon V
Murder Under A Black Moon VI
Murder Under A Full Moon VII
Murder Under A New Moon VIII

Last Chance For Love Romance Series
Last Chance Motel I
Gasping For Air II
The Siren's Call III
Hard Landing IV
The Mermaid's Carol V

PROLOGUE

"**Y**ou're arresting me?"

"Josiah, please don't make this any harder. Detective Drake is hoping you will resist, so he can pile on more charges."

I was stunned. Of all the people they could have sent to arrest me, it would be Detective Kelly, the high school boyfriend of my daughter, Asa. He practically lived at my house when he was a boy. "What's the charge?"

"Accessory to second-degree murder," an embarrassed Kelly answered, sweat trickling down his temple.

"MURDER!" I shouted. "No way!"

"I'm sorry, Josiah, but I've got to take you in. Please turn around so I can cuff you."

"You're cuffing me? I am sorry that I ever befriended you, Kelly. You're a snake." I was so indignant I could have spit nickels. Suddenly I got an idea and clasped my chest. "I feel funny. I think I'm having a heart attack." Having said that, I tumbled to the ground.

"Josiah! Josiah!" Kelly yelled at the officer hanging

back by the police cruiser. "Call for an ambulance! Hurry!" He knelt beside me to feel for a pulse. "You better not die on me. Asa will kill me. You hear me. Oh, gawd! You better be faking." Kelly shook me. "Are you faking, Josiah?"

I stifled a smile. You better believe I was faking it. There was no way I was going to let Kelly cart me off in a police car to jail. This entire mess started when I helped a farmers' market friend get some bullies off his back. You know how much I hate bullies. Now, I'm being arrested for murder! How did that happen?

Let me introduce myself for those of you who don't know me. My name is Josiah Reynolds. I'm in my fifties, had a terrible accident some years back and now walk with a slight limp and wear a hearing aid. I'll tell you about my accident later. I live in the Butterfly, a mid-century marvel, that hovers on a precipice above the Kentucky River. I used to be an art history professor, but now I make my living as a beekeeper. I also board horses on my farm and own a catering firm, renting out the Butterfly for events.

I say that I'm a widow, but the truth of the matter is my husband and I were in the midst of a nasty divorce when he up and died on me. He had run off with a socialite our daughter's age and fathered a love child with her. That didn't hurt as much as the fact he stole our entire savings and hid it. I almost went bankrupt and nearly lost the farm. I never did recover our savings. It took years to climb out of debt, but I did it. I guess I could sell the Butterfly and the farm, but I worry about developers. They are swallowing up one precious horse farm after another, and with it, our culture. Do we really need another mall?

The problem is compounded by people moving to the Bluegrass with no knowledge of our fragile ecosystem and history. They don't give a hoot about these farms, the workers they employ, how much money these farms pump into the local economy, or the tourists they draw. I bet two out of three people don't even know the Bluegrass is bordered on the south by the Kentucky River and a cliff system called the Palisades.

I digress. I could go on and on about this subject, but I won't bore you with it further.

Let's get back to why I'm being arrested. I told you that I was helping a friend. What do I get for my trouble—thrown into the back of a police car.

Well, you know what they say—no good deed goes unpunished!

1

This whole thing started some months previously when I followed the curious crowd to a melee on the south side of the farmers' market upon hearing a ruckus near the street. You can't imagine my surprise when I see two men pummeling my buddy, Rodney Hiller, who has a booth next to mine. I thought he had left his booth to use the *Gents,* and here he was brawling with two men half his age.

Instead of intervening to stop the fight, people were standing around and recording it on their phones. And you wonder why I can't stand people.

Irene Meckler, the flower lady, and I pushed through the crowd to stop the fight. I grabbed the younger guy's arm as he was about to swing at Rodney again. "Break it up! Break it up!"

The man swirled around and was about to punch me when Baby, my English Mastiff, rushed between us. My two hundred pound dog gave the man pause, especially when Baby flashed his fangs. Thank goodness the man backed off because I have a glass jaw.

By this time, the market manager pressed through the crowd and called the police for help. The other farmers left their booths, creating a little circle around us. The two young men, knowing they were outnumbered, stopped pounding poor Rodney.

Here's the truth about farmers in farmers' markets. We fight and cuss at each other all the time, usually at board meetings. However, we draw the line with outsiders beating us up. The market manager photographed the two men as they tried unsuccessfully to grab his phone. Fearing the police, the young men ran to their little table and furiously tried to pack up. Rodney and the manager followed, so another fisticuffs broke out as sirens wailed in the distance.

To add to the confusion, there was a man circling the men while recording the whole shebang.

Well, I love a good fight as well as the next person, but this was too much even for me. I watched from the sideline as the police pushed everyone apart. The market manager and Rodney talked to one officer and the two young men talked to another. The two young men must not have been convincing because they were handcuffed and led away.

Everyone clapped.

The police confiscated the expensive Kentucky agate on the men's table. One beautiful cut slab fell off the table and broke apart. I grimaced, knowing that the broken shards were not worth as much as when they had been one whole slab of agate.

The police asked the farmers to go back to their booths. They didn't have to ask twice as the farmers were losing sales not being at their stalls.

Irene and I drifted back to our booths as the police talked to Rod. I took it upon myself to watch Rod's booth as well, but there was one problem. I didn't know how to correctly weigh tomatoes on his new digital scales, but I gave it my best shot.

Finally, Rod straggled back to his booth.

"You look like hell, Rod."

He pulled a comb out of his shirt pocket and pulled it through his salt and pepper hair. A button was missing from his thin striped maroon shirt and his good work boots were scuffed up.

"Who pulled the first punch?"

"The older one with the Pittsburgh Pirates baseball cap." Rodney twisted his mouth and felt his jaw. "I think a tooth is loose." He looked despondent. "I just had my teeth fixed, too."

"Those goons looked pretty ragged, so you must have gotten in some punches, too."

Rod smirked. "Punks, both of them. If I see either one of them again, I'll kill 'em."

"Don't say stuff like that. Bad karma."

"You never wanted someone killed? I seem to re-member there were two men you wanted dead and buried."

I snickered, "And look where it got me."

"Yeah, they're both six feet under now."

"Sometimes the universe smiles upon me."

We both guffawed.

We were not laughing because we thought death is funny. We were laughing at the irony of it. Some folks are rotten to the core. I should know. I've run into a few of them. And yes, I confess I wanted them dead, but I didn't cause them to be dead. There's a difference in "wanting" and "causing."

Rodney winced, feeling his jaw again. "I'm too old for this kind of baloney."

"What was it about?"

"First of all, those boys had no right to set up a table and sell. They are not a part of the market."

"I know, but why not let the manager handle it?"

"Did you see what they were selling?"

"Kentucky agate."

"Not just any agate. They were selling *my* agate."

"What!" I said.

"Last week someone broke into my workshop and stole over five thousand dollars worth of my best agate."

"I didn't know. You never said. That's terrible, Rod."

Rod is the most famous agate hunter in the state. I would say even in the United States. He regularly sells to jewelry designers across the country, has written books, and even appeared on TV shows discussing rare Kentucky agate.

Agate is a crystalline variety of mineral quartz with varying colors arranged in layers. Agate with red is the most prized and is caused by iron while blue is caused by manganese. It is used for jewelry and other ornamental uses.

"Yeah, Josiah, and guess who the dirty skunks were? Those boys took my agate. I saw my mark on the pieces they were selling."

"Can you prove *they* stole it?"

Rod looked at me as though I were daft. "How else would they have my agate in their possession? You didn't see them pull out a bill of sale, did you?"

I was thrown for a loop. It was pretty brazen for thieves to unload their loot in such close proximity to their victim. Perhaps they didn't know Rod sold at the farmers' market. How stupid can one be? "True. Very true. Do you know them?"

"They're the Statler brothers from down my way, and they've been nothing but trouble since the day they were born. Born bad, pure and simple."

"I see, but I don't understand why they would set up selling agate where you work on Saturdays."

"To intimidate and rile me up. Did you see that man with the fancy camera filming the fight?"

"Yeah, I did notice him."

"These boys are newbie rock hounds. They made

their name by salting streams and then claiming to be genius rock hunters. They paid someone to film them discovering gold and precious minerals in Kentucky and became a huge hit on YouTube and something called TikTok."

I laughed. "There's no gold in Kentucky."

"Exactly! They got called out on that, so now they've moved on to agate, which Kentucky is known for. It's even the official state rock. Look, Josiah, rock hunting is becoming the new 'thing.' Kentucky contains fluorspar, quartz veins, and large quantities of fresh water pearls, fossils, and agate. These bozos are just trying to get ahead of the curve on this latest hobby wave."

"But what has that got to do with you?"

"I swear those brothers have been stalking me. I just saw one of their videos where they were hunting in my favorite stream for agate. Now, I've kept that stream site a secret for over twenty years and they just stumble upon it? No, ma'am. They followed me and stole my site."

I could see the problem. Prices for agate were going through the roof. My own kitchen back splash was made from the mineral which Rod provided, and I had huge chunky agate necklaces which were now quite valuable. It seemed a shame that years after Rod had invested in making agate popular, he was going to be shortchanged when he could finally make some real money off the mineral.

I had gone with Rod on several hunting expeditions, and the man had a keen eye for hunting geodes. I liked the sport—strolling through shallow creeks filled with cold water. I must admit though, I found more pleasure in spotting the fish, tadpoles, and other life in the water rather than seeking rocks, but the entire experience was fun.

"I guarantee you, Josiah, there will be a video up this very day of the fight, making these boys more popular than ever. You wait and see!"

It turned out Rod was right.

Some people have no shame.

2

When I got home to the Butterfly, my mid-century marvel, I emptied my VW van, which had been recently renovated. I had a few bottles of honey left, and I wanted to get them out of the hot vehicle into a cooler space. After that I checked on my bees.

One hive looked to be struggling. There were only a few guard bees around the entrance, so I pushed the hive forward with my knee. The hive tilted forward, feeling light. That meant trouble. Hives should not move with the knee test. I needed to get inside and see what the matter was, but I would do it later when I was fresh. Putting on a suit and lighting a smoker seemed too much at the moment. I was too tired to fool with them.

I went to check on the pastures. Since it was getting dark, I brought in the boarded horses. I don't like to leave them outside overnight because of the coyotes, especially mares with foals. I opened the gates from the pastures to the barn, calling for them while pounding on a feed bucket. They came helter skelter knowing the sound of the bucket meant a sweet treat of a honey and oat mixture. They gave me no problem.

The other pastoral animals I don't worry about being outside because donkeys are with them in the fields. Donkeys are very brave when it comes to coyotes, but they don't get along with the horses—at least, not with the high-strung Thoroughbred horses. Thoroughbreds are partial to goats.

Going back to the Butterfly, I put my free-range chickens in their cage, as I like to keep the chickens close to the house. Their home is near my bedroom so I can keep an eye on them at night or, at least, hear if they squawk. I have a mama fox and her kits who would love to snack on my chickens.

The barn cats—the Kitty Kaboodle—came inside the house, much to Baby's delight after he brought his bowl over to me. The cats were Baby's pets and slept with him in my room until morning when they were let out for the day.

Baby dropped the bowl at my feet.

"Jeez, let me take off my shoes first, Baby." I was tired, and truth be told, I was rattled after seeing the fight at the farmers' market. I guess I had seen enough violence in the last several years.

Baby nudged me with his muzzle.

Ignoring his droopy face, I changed my clothes and went into the bathroom to wash my face. Baby padded after me with the cats scampering after him. "All right! All right! You are such a pest—all of you!" In order to get some peace, I went to the kitchen and fed Baby and the meowing felines. While they munched happily, I put fresh water in their bowls before pouring myself a small bourbon neat. Leaning against the kitchen counter, I ran my hands over the smooth, polished agate backsplash. It was gorgeous, and I was glad I had spent the extra money on it.

Taking a few sips of my Kentucky-made firewater, I watched the animals eat and drink, thinking the house was too quiet. The silence reminded me of a tomb. I realized I didn't like coming home to an empty house after a long day at the farmers' market. Matt, my best friend, was in California with baby Emmeline, visiting the child's bi-polar mother. Franklin, my other close friend, was busy with his life. My boyfriend, Hunter, was still out-of-town working. My daughter, Asa, was God-knows-where.

I decided to drop in on my next-door neighbor, Lady Elsmere, and invite myself to dinner. She wouldn't mind.

Changing my clothes for something more presentable, I painted on some makeup and combed my hair. Pleased with my appearance, I made my way to the Big House, a mansion built in 1839, which my late husband restored to its former glory after Lady Elsmere purchased the dilapidated mansion and farm next door.

Never my custom to knock, I let myself in the kitchen where Bess DuPuy was busy cooking. She looked up in surprise. "What are you doing here?"

"I thought I'd join Her Ladyship for dinner."

"That's presumptuous of you."

I was taken aback by Bess' sharp words. My showing up for dinner unannounced had been a standing practice with Lady Elsmere, aka June Webster of Monkey's Eyebrow, for years now. Why was tonight any different?

My expression must have shown my surprise. I was never very good at hiding my emotions, which is why I'm such a lousy poker player. "Something of note happened at the farmers' market today. I thought she might like to know."

Bess looked chagrined. "I'm sorry, Josiah. I didn't mean to be so sharp. Miss June is having a dinner party tonight, and I'm shorthanded."

So you don't get confused, we call Lady Elsmere her Christian name in private. The staff adds the salutation Miss—or not, depending on their mood—but we all refer to her as Lady Elsmere in public. After her first husband died, June married Lord Elsmere, a wealthy, eccentric peer of the British realm. He has long since been deceased, and June came back home to Kentucky with her title and wealth intact.

"I didn't know. May I help you?" I thought it unusual that June would have a party and I not know about it.

"It's just the family with Miss June. She wants to make some sort of announcement. It's making me nervous, and I'm behind on the dinner."

"What do you think it's about?"

"I'm thinking it's about the will. I'm wondering if she's changed her mind about Daddy being her heir and switching it back to Lord Elsmere's nephew, Anthony."

Bess' father was Charles DuPuy, who started out as June's butler and had graduated to managing her estate and proclaimed as her heir. I had talked June into making the DuPuy family her heirs as she had no children, and, frankly, I thought the family deserved it. They had worked like dogs for her.

"I can't see that. June's said nothing to me about it. Besides, Anthony has already signed an agreement that he wouldn't contest your family as June's heirs when she gave him that settlement. He's entitled to Lord Elsmere's estate in England and the title that goes with it, but he can't touch June's money or property in the States." I looked about the messy kitchen and took a deep breath. The kitchen smelled divine.

I grinned. "Look, let me help first, then fix me a plate to take home. I won't make this offer again."

Bess smiled. "Can you set the dining room table?"

I nodded.

"Use the bone china and the Waterford wine and water goblets."

"Formal, huh. How many forks?"

Bess thought for a moment. "Three. Salad, entrée, and dessert."

"Napkins?"

"The white linen ones embroidered with Lord Elsmere's family crest."

"Will do."

Bess checked the oven while I made a beeline to the formal dining room and set about to work. It took me twenty minutes to set the table for eight people—Lady Elsmere, Charles and Josephine DuPuy, their two daughters, Bess and Amelia, and Charles' three grandsons—Malcolm, Tyrone, and Aaron.

Bess brought in a fresh-cut flower arrangement to set on the table. We both stood back, admiring the dining room with its expensive damask wallpaper, gleaming antiques, polished sterling silverware, and sparkling crystal goblets.

"You're really puttin' on the Ritz, Bess."

"If we're going to be disinherited, I want to go out in style."

"June is doing no such thing. You're being hysterical."

"I hope you're right, but June's been talking with her lawyers all this week, including Matt."

"Hmm. Matt left for California yesterday with the baby. He won't be back for a week." I didn't know what else to say. June usually told me everything, but hadn't said a hoot about seeing her lawyers.

"I've got to change. I've laid a basket out for you, Josiah. Thank you very much. The table looks grand."

I nodded and left as I could see Bess was distracted. I picked up the picnic basket which was heavy, so I borrowed one of June's many golf carts to lug it home. I would return the basket and golf cart tomorrow morning, hopefully seeing June and getting the low-down on the dinner party.

As soon as I was back inside the Butterfly, I headed for my office where I turned on my computer. From the basket, I pulled out containers filled with a fresh tomato and cucumber salad, lobster soup, grilled trout, and fried milk corn with summer squash. I then turned on YouTube and searched for the low-down, no-count agate stealing Statler brothers.

It was just as Rod predicted. There was a new video posted by the brothers deftly edited showing Rod as the instigator abusing these "poor lads" who just wanted to sell their agate at the farmers' market. No context at all about selling Rod's stolen agate illegally at the market and causing mayhem in general. The video had been uploaded three hours ago and already had over twenty thousand views.

I stuffed trout into my mouth. Hmm. Baked to perfection. I expected nothing less of Bess. She was a true artist when it came to food. Even though nauseated watching the Statler's videos, it didn't stop me from finishing my dinner, including an extra large slice of lemon meringue pie.

The Statler brothers had a large following of viewers. I found it creepy that they had filmed in several of Rod's secret hunting holes, which I recognized.

Also, Rod was a Civil War reenactor. So were they. Rod was a pre-1875 musket, carbine, and rifle expert. They claimed to be also. It was like they were trying to usurp Rod's life—stealing it right from under him.

Finally turning off my computer, I leaned back in my chair. Something was not right with these young men. I found their behavior toward Rod to be unnerving, hostile, and unbalanced.

I wondered what caused such aggression toward Rod. Did it come out of nowhere? I didn't think so. Kentucky is known for its blood feuds.

Was Rod was lying to me?

It wouldn't be the first time a man had lied to me.

3

I got up early. After feeding Baby and the Kitty Kaboodle, I traipsed over to the Big House by driving through the pastures. Malcolm, Charles' grandson, had already been over to let my boarded horses out. I looked at my watch. It was 7:30. Horse people are early risers.

Last year June and I had shared the cost of installing electronic gates between her farm and mine, since she sometimes uses my barn for her overflow of horses. The gates opened for me as I sailed right through. It was lovely.

Finally reaching the Big house, I stopped the golf cart beside the others and climbed out with an empty basket in hand. As with my usual practice, I entered the mansion through the kitchen door and put the basket on the table. "Good morning, Bess."

"I suppose you want breakfast now?"

"Ooh, cranky are we?" I said, giving her a quick kiss on her cheek. Noticing that Bess' brown eyes were puffy and red, I swung her around. "Bess, what's the matter?"

"You know what that crazy old woman did last night?"

I stepped back feeling my heart freeze. "June didn't disinherit your family, did she?"

Bess put both her hands on my shoulders and gave me a little shake. "Josiah, she gave us each a million dollars last night."

"What!"

Bess took a check from her ample bosom and handed it to me. "Here, look."

"I'm not touching that thing after being stuck between your mammary glands."

"I don't know about your titties, but mine are bathed and powdered daily."

"Okay, okay. Let's see." I took the check and whistled. It was a check for a million dollars signed by June as Lady Elsmere. It was indeed her scrawling signature.

I gave Bess a hug. "Congratulations, Bess! What are you going to do with the money?"

"Put it in the bank."

"How dull." I handed back the check, which Bess promptly transferred to the security of her ample bosom.

When she saw my disapproving look, Bess said, "Nobody is gonna steal this check before I hit the bank."

I nodded. "Believe me when I say that check is safer than the gold in Fort Knox."

Bess twisted her lips, making a face.

"So tell me. Are you going to retire now?"

"I'm gonna buy myself a new car. Some new clothes. Travel a little bit, but for the most part, I'll go on cooking for the Big House. I don't like strangers in my kitchen."

"You are not a mere cook. You are a chef—a master chef of Southern cuisine. Other celebrity chefs should bow at your feet. That trout melted in my mouth last night."

Bess smiled. "Did it?"

"Yes, ma'am. I was a Girl Scout, so I cannot tell a lie."

"Fish is tricky, you know." Bess turned to her gas range and began cracking eggs.

"How did the rest of the family react?"

"Amelia, Mom, and I screamed with joy and immediately began crying. I haven't stopped since."

"Charles?"

"Daddy didn't say much. He was real quiet."

"I guess it was the shock. What about the boys?" I was speaking of the three grandsons.

"Their money has been put in a special account. They will receive a stipend every month as long as they are working full time or going to school. The money is to pay for their education and reasonable transportation. No Lamborghinis. They will receive the bulk of it when they hit thirty."

"I think that was very wise of June. If those boys were able to get their hands on the money now, they would blow it on cars and girls."

"I know. I was very grateful June set it up like that. Takes temptation off the table."

Bess prepared a tray with two plates of sunny side up eggs, toast, country ham, cheese grits, and fluffy biscuits covered with red-eye gravy. She handed the tray to me. "Take this up to Her Ladyship. The second plate is for you. I'll bring the coffee up in a minute."

"May I have a glass of milk?" I was not partial to coffee.

"Don't push your luck, Josiah."

A bell rang.

Bess looked up. "She is up and hungry. Get going before my perfect eggs get cold."

I gave the eggs a cursory glance as they were from my chickens. They did indeed look pleasing to the eye with their bright orange yolks standing at attention. Picking up the tray, I passed through the grand foyer where the elevator stood and pushed the second floor button with my knuckle. Groaning, the elevator made its way up. I got out and hurried to June's bedroom, making sure the tray stayed level. Luckily, her door was opened.

Lady Elsmere was sitting up in bed wearing a lavender, quilted satin bed jacket from the 1950s. She was also in full makeup, wearing one of her several diamond tiaras on her white hair, which was tied back in a chignon. She had her eyes glued to a steamy romance novel with a half-naked man on the cover.

I laughed.

"I heard you chatting up Bess downstairs."

"You sure look pretty fancy so early in the morning, especially after last night."

June looked inquisitively at me. "Bess told you?"

"Yes, very generous of you."

"Tosh. Why do old rich people sit on their money until they die? Money is to be spent and given to loved ones to enjoy while they still can. I'm not going to travel anymore and my needs are simple now. I have everything. All I want for my remaining years is to be comfortable and not endure any pain before my passing."

"Oh, shut up." I placed the tray across her lap. "Since you are so eager to die, eat this. The cholesterol from this breakfast alone will surely clog your arteries. No doubt, you'll die of a heart attack. That ought to make you happy."

"I see you're having a cholesterol, heart attack breakfast as well."

"Yes, and I can't wait to dive in."

Bess walked in with a tray of coffee, milk, and hot tea. "Heard that." She placed the tray on the nightstand

and poured June a cup of steaming black coffee.

"I don't see how anyone can drink that stuff," I said.

Bess pulled a chair up to the bedside and unfolded a small tablecloth on the edge of the bed before placing my extra plate of food on it. "Sit, Josiah, and don't get anything on Miss June's bedspread. Amelia just had it cleaned."

"I promise," I said, sitting in the chair and pulling it closer to the bed.

"Can you stay with Miss June while I run to the bank?" Bess asked me.

"Sure."

June took a sip of her coffee. "Ah, I feel human again." She called after Bess, who was leaving, "Make sure you deal with the bank manager himself. He's expecting y'all today."

"Yes, Miss June."

We heard Bess descend to the main floor in the elevator.

"Where is everyone?" I asked.

"At the bank depositing their checks, I suppose."

I repeated my praise of June's thoughtful bequest to the DuPuy family. "That was very kind of you."

June dismissed my comment with a wave of her hand. "Money is like manure. Should be spread around or it stinks."

"That's one way of looking at it."

"Enough talk about money. I've been reading about the DuPuy family. You know Charles' ancestor was Aaron DuPuy, a slave of Henry Clay's. Grew up with him from childhood."

"Yes, I told you that years ago. Eat your breakfast before it gets cold, June."

"Well, as I was saying, Miss Know-It-All, quite a bit of history has been buried. Aaron and Charlotte, his wife, were taken by Henry Clay to Washington D. C. when Clay was Secretary of State. There, Charlotte sued Clay for her freedom."

"Again, I told you that years ago. She left the Clay household and lived as a free woman in Washington awaiting her trial. However, Charlotte lost her case and was sent back as a slave to Kentucky. That must have been a bitter pill to swallow."

June pondered, "Exactly. I wonder how Charlotte's relationship with Aaron was after that."

"Acrimonious I would guess."

"You should know. You're an embittered woman, period."

I ignored June's jab, cutting into my eggs. She had taken to attacking me from time to time recently. I don't know why.

"He did not join her in the lawsuit and came back voluntarily to Kentucky with Clay."

I said, "That is if Aaron did go back voluntarily. The law was on Henry Clay's side, and Aaron had their children, who were still slaves, to think about. Regardless, I could see how Charlotte might have thought Aaron's relationship with Clay was stronger than his love for her. You know Aaron saw Charlotte on a neighboring plantation and had Clay buy her for him."

Ignoring my remarks, June continued to lecture. "Everyone remembers Harriet Tubman, but Charlotte DuPuy had been just as brave. Imagine taking on Henry Clay, the greatest statesman the U.S. has ever produced. It's a shame there is no statue of this woman in Lexington. She not only stood up to the issue of slavery, but to male dominance over her life. Charlotte was a heroic woman—ahead of her time. I think she is the main reason that Clay's bids for the presidency failed. It's sad no one knows about her now."

I said, "You've got the money. Commission a statue of her."

"I don't know what she looked like, but I got this." She reached into the nightstand drawer and pulled out an old daguerreotype of a black man with gray hair. She handed it to me.

"Who's this?"

"That is the only surviving picture of Aaron DuPuy, Charles' ancestor. I think it was taken after Henry Clay's death."

I looked at the photo. "This is amazing. Are you going to give it to Charles?"

"Maybe for his birthday."

"He'll love it." I handed the daguerreotype back.

June put the picture back into the drawer. "Now tell me what's been going on with you. I heard there was a little tussle at the farmers' market yesterday."

I was astonished. "Is there anything you don't know? You must have spies everywhere."

"You flatter me."

"Well, these yahoos from Lincoln County set up shop selling agate, which Rod Hiller claims was stolen from him weeks earlier."

"Was it?"

"Looks like it. Some of the larger pieces had Rod's markings on the back. I saw for myself."

June cut into her biscuit. "What happened?"

"Rod recognized the agate and confronted them. A fight ensued. The police were called, and the thieves were arrested. End of story."

"What were their names again?"

"Their last name is Statler. They are in their twenties, maybe early thirties, I would say about."

June frowned, awkwardly playing with her food. "Curry and Skeeter Statler?"

"Yeah, that's them."

"I see. I might know their family. If their daddy is Jimmy Ray Statler, he worked on my farm when I first bought it. I had to fire him."

"Over what?"

"Equipment parts went missing, especially for the

tractors and other big machinery."

"Small world."

"Charles would remember him."

"I'll see if I can track Charles down before I leave."

"He's probably in town at the bank."

I shrugged. "I guess there's no hurry on this. It's Rod's problem—not mine."

"That's right. Don't go sticking your nose in other people's business. AGAIN!"

I chuckled. "You should talk. You're the biggest *buttinsky* ever."

June kidded, "Ah, shucks. You make me blush."

The verbal jousting over, I returned to my breakfast.

June sighed and put down her fork. "I'm done. Take the tray away, Josiah."

"You haven't even touched your eggs."

"I'm not hungry."

I scolded, "You eat those eggs, old woman. You need the protein. I'm not leaving until you do."

June complained, "Tyrant."

"And some ham, too. Woman shall not live on biscuits and gravy alone."

June dabbed her extra biscuit into the perfectly cooked orange yolks. She looked at me with surprise. "These are very good. Bess salted them just right."

I didn't say anything because I knew Bess had not salted them. There was no point in correcting her. My heart dropped a little bit. I realized June was getting worse, but didn't want to think of her passing. She was like a mother to me, and I couldn't bear the thought of losing her.

I love that cantankerous old biddy!

4

I guess the real trouble started with the Civil War reenactment dry run. June was underwriting the reenactment as well as the ball that same evening. Don't ask me why. I thought it was folly.

Eunice, Franklin, and I went to the practice taking place on June's second farm, where she housed retired race horses and other abandoned animals. It was just down the road from our farms. It was necessary to remove the animals, so June had them transferred to the Big House pastures and other excess livestock to my farm.

What a strange band of friends the three of us made wandering about the Civil War campsite. Eunice's ancestors had fled to Camp Nelson, Kentucky, where African-Americans signed up for the Union Army, even though they were still technically slaves. My ancestor signed up for the Union Army in Cincinnati in the year of Our Lord 1863. I have pictures of my great-great-grandfather looking terrified in his corporal uniform. He looked about sixteen. Later he was photographed as a sergeant with his commanding officers. In that picture, he looked like an old man. Franklin was the odd man out. His ancestors supported the Confederacy. Wickliffe Farm, Franklin's ancestral home, had been a plantation that raised hemp and livestock tended by slaves.

Yet, we three wandered around the makeshift military encampment, poking our noses inside sutler tents that specialized in selling Civil War equipment and uniforms, between bouts of watching reenactors practice shooting their muskets.

"Here, Josiah, look at this dress. It's perfect for the ball," Franklin said, swiping a blue dress with white ruffles off a rack in front of a tent that sold women's nineteenth-century apparel.

"I am not going to wear a period dress," I said. "I hate those hooped frocks. You can't go to the bathroom in them. Besides, I will be helping Eunice with the catering." Eunice and I were in a catering business together. She had run a boutique hotel in the Bahamas and knew everything there was to know about the hospitality industry.

"I was invited to the ball as a guest," Eunice said, going through the rack. "And I'm going."

"Who's going to run the kitchen? We were paid a lot of money for this shindig."

"Oh, ye of little faith, I've got it covered. I promised

Sharlene half of my cut plus her regular pay if she would run this little affair and make sure everything runs smoothly. She jumped at the chance." Sharlene was a middle-aged woman and a homemaker with no work record, whom we hired several years ago. She turned out to be one of our best employees.

"I see." I was a little disappointed as I didn't really want to be a guest at this ball. People get riled up about the Civil War. Kentucky never seceded from the Union, but politically, it was split down the middle. Anytime there is a discussion about the Civil War, it gets heated because we are still facing many of the same issues people faced in the war. I didn't like to be around such a minefield.

I'm all about the present and the future. I always say—"Let the dead bury the dead." Let's move forward to make the world better. Why concentrate on old grudges, but since June was sponsoring the reenactment and the ball afterward, I was expected to go.

"Whom are you going as?"

"No one in particular," I replied.

"I'm going as Mary Bowser. She was a Union spy working as a servant in Jeff Davis' home in Richmond."

"Was she a slave?"

"She was a free black woman posing as a slave. She had a photographic memory and could report detailed information gleaned from reports on Davis' desk."

"Never heard of her."

Eunice pulled out an orange taffeta dress and asked the clerk if she could try it on.

"You're gonna look like a pumpkin in that thing," I called after her.

Eunice ignored me as she entered the improvised dressing room.

Franklin thrust the blue dress at me. "Go after her and try this on. It's a perfect color with your red hair."

"How am I to even put this thing on by myself?" I questioned, looking at the authentic-looking hooks and loops in the back.

"I'll come over early and help you. Now git, girl."

"What are you going to wear?"

"I have several authentic uniforms to choose from tucked neatly away in tissue paper in the attic."

"Well, fiddle de de."

Bemused, Franklin thrust the silk dress at me again and shook it.

"Oh, all right. I hope this makes you happy, Johnny Reb." I grabbed the dress and entered a makeshift dressing room. I threw the dress over my clothes and admired myself in the mirror, twisting to get the best advantage. I had to admit I did look good. Okay, I was sold. I took it off and went to look for the saleslady when I met Eunice going through the rack again. "Well?"

"I did look like a pumpkin."

I replied, "Told ya."

"How about this yellow one?"

I shook my head. "Will clash with your skin color. You need a dress that brings out the pretty tones in your skin." Eunice's skin was a warm caramel color.

My skin was pale—too pale for my liking. I sometimes looked like a ghost in the mirror. No one had to tell me twice that I came from Viking stock with my white skin, green eyes, and red hair. "Here, take this dress," I said, handing it over to Eunice. "You'd look good in this color, and it's low cut. You can show off your *assets*."

"What about you?"

"I'll take this black one. I'll go as the Merry Widow." I pulled out the mourning dress and held it up. "How do I look?"

"Is the Merry Widow any kin to the Black Widow?" Franklin asked, rummaging through the petticoats and crotchless lady pantaloons.

"Is that a rhetorical question?" I asked.

Franklin turned to the clerk. "What about the hoops?"

"We have the newest hoops, sir. Very flexible."

"What about sitting?"

"Very comfortable."

"What about private matters?"

"If need be the hoop can easily snap off, be removed, and then quickly put back on under the skirt in a matter of seconds."

"See, Josiah. You can sit and pee in comfort," Franklin said. "All you have to do is snap, unsnap, and then resnap. Easy peasy." He handed me the undergarments and petticoats needed for the dress as well as the hoop.

"I'll wear a crinoline, but not a hoop. There's something about a hoop I can't abide."

Franklin said, "They were designed to keep the dress fabric away from women's legs and from under their feet, so they wouldn't trip."

"I don't care. I'm not wearing one. You can't move in them." I snatched the other garments from Franklin's hand and grudgingly paid for them. While I was waiting for Eunice to make up her mind about which dress to select, I sat on a bench outside the costume tent when I caught a glimpse of Curry and Skeeter Statler strolling down a gentle hill toward the Union campsite. I had forgotten their website stated they were Civil War reenactors. I felt a sudden chill.

I glanced over and saw Rod setting up his pup tent as were other "Union" soldiers. Afterward, they would cook a meal over an open fire and sleep in the meadow as did their ancestors.

Curry and Skeeter made a beeline for Rod.

I knew in my bones they were going to cause trouble. "Here, hold these," I said to Franklin, tossing my packages toward him.

"Where are you going?" Franklin yelled.

I can't run very fast as I have a limp, due to an accident years ago, but I can manage a fast walk. I arrived just in time to hear Skeeter berate Rod for getting them arrested.

Rod reiterated, "You boys stole my agate. It's undeniable."

Curry said, "You get those charges dropped or you'll be sorry."

"You can't come around here and threaten me."

Skeeter stepped forward and poked Rod in the chest. "You better listen to us, old man."

"You touch me again, and you'll be lying in a gutter dead somewhere," Rod said, stepping closer to Skeeter.

Skeeter's eyes widened in surprise. He wasn't expecting Rod to be so combative after their last confrontation.

One of Rod's comrades pulled out a phone and started recording the altercation. As soon as the Statler brothers realized they were being filmed, they smiled and waved to the phone, making a pitch to watch them on YouTube. Then they quickly walked away.

"What did they want?" I asked Rod, who turned toward me after thanking his fellow comrades.

"Trash talk. They've been following me since that day at the market and making no bones about it. I see their truck behind me when I go into town. If I go into a diner to get something to eat, they come in ten minutes later. I even see them hanging out in my church parking lot."

I commiserated as I'd had my own stalker in the past. He's the one that caused my accident where I fell off a cliff. The only thing that stopped me from plunging into the Kentucky River a hundred feet below was getting snagged on a small outcropping on the way down. "It's too bad Kentucky has such crappy stalking laws. Did you notify the police?"

"They won't do nothing unless they attack me again."

"Didn't Skeeter poke you and your friend-in-arms film it? Take that to the DA. At least make a police report."

Rod tipped back his kepi hat. "I just might at that. My buddy, Saginaw, filmed it." He waved at someone who called his name passing by. "Enough of this hooey, what are you doing here?"

"Came to buy a dress for the ball tomorrow night. I've been commanded to attend by Lady Elsmere."

"It was great of Her Ladyship to sponsor this event." Rod looked around making sure that the Statler boys hadn't circled back on him.

"Rod, why do you do this?"

"Do what?"

"Be a Civil War reenactor?" I looked about at all the people wearing military uniforms, putting up tents, tending to horses, cooking over an open fire, and cleaning their weaponry. There must have been over two hundred men milling about.

Rod squinted and wiped his sweating brow with a bandana. "Everybody's got a different reason. Some do it to honor their ancestors. See that tall African-American feller chatting with the Union soldiers over there?"

"Yes."

"We call him Shooby. He comes every year to cheer us on, but doesn't participate because he's a particular reenactor. He only participates in USCT battles."

"What's that?"

"They were the United States Colored Troops."

"Oh."

"Approximately 179,000 black men served as soldiers in the U.S. Army while another 19,000 served in the Navy. By the end of the Cival War, 40,000 black soldiers died due to battle action and another 30,000 men died of disease or infections. Many of them signed up at Camp Nelson, not too far from here as the crow flies."

"That I knew, but I didn't realize so many slaves had fought on the Union side."

"Not all of them were slaves. Freed African-American men fought as well. Remember the film *Glory* with Morgan Freeman and Denzel Washington? That's about the USCT."

"I'll have to watch it again."

"Shooby's great-great-grandfather fought in the USCT, so Shooby reenacts to honor those ancestors, who sacrificed before him. It's his way of saying thank you. That's one story." Rod pointed to another man who was cleaning his brogans. "That feller over there thinks he is the reincarnation of a Civil War soldier who died in battle. Nothing you say will cause him to doubt that he was a young man who died in the Perryville mêlée. Of course, he's a little baffled about which side he was fighting on."

Perryville was the bloodiest battle in Kentucky during 1862 with sixteen thousand Confederates fighting against fifty-five thousand Federal troops. Statistics vary, but there were approximately 7,637 casualties with 1,355 dead divided between the two sides. It was the South's last attempt to gain possession of Kentucky. I knew that Rod always participated in the reenactment of it.

"You're joshing me. He can't remember which side he fought on?"

"I'm dead serious." Rod pointed to another man putting whole potatoes under hot coals of his fire. "That feller does it to get away from his nag of a wife. Everyone has a different reason. We also have Native Americans, women, Hispanics who fight as well."

"Women?"

"It is estimated that 750 women disguised themselves and fought as bravely as any man. There's Sarah

Seelye, who received a veteran's pension, and Jennie Hodgers who fought in forty engagements, just to name a few. We'll have women fighting with us tomorrow."

"But why do *you* do it?"

"That's a discussion for another time," Rod said, winking.

"Come on, Rod."

"It's personal with me—what I believe about this great country of ours. We've fought for our freedom. Bled for our freedom. I think it is important that we don't forget the horrors of the Civil War, or we are aimed to repeat it. I really believe in E Pluribus Unum."

"Out of many—one."

"Kentucky has a similar motto. *United we stand. Divided we fall.* I think that is an ideal we need to cling to—all of us, no matter of race, creed, sex, or religion. We have more in common than not. We must remember that."

"That brings up my next question."

"Shoot."

"How do you keep politics out of it?"

"It's very simple. We just do. Each soldier must buy an outfit for both sides. There are times when reenactors have to switch armies because the numbers are not correct. If your commanding officer tells you to take off your Union uniform and put on the grays, you do it without question. If you pitch a fit, you're booted out.

We're here to remember history and honor the past—not to debate the pros and cons of the war. We leave that to historians."

Rod continued to talk in length about the battle tomorrow.

I was astounded at the complexity of Civil War reenactments. I discovered that each "soldier" must enlist as a private and can only improve his/her rank by taking detailed tests, drilling, and showing knowledge of weapons and equipment used during that time period. There were different kinds of reenactors—mainstream, campaigners, and stitch counters. The stitch counters are the more serious of the actors. They know Civil War history down to the smallest detail, even how a uniform was manufactured—thus the nickname.

There are different types of events as well—invitation or immersion. This weekend was an invitation event.

I asked Rod why he thought the North won when the South had such spectacular generals.

"Technology," he answered. "Union troops began using the 1860 Henry repeating rifle and carbine or the Spencer. Those guns had thirteen shots while the muskets are single shots."

"I didn't think the Union Army supplied that many Henrys as they were so expensive."

"They supplied enough. The Confederates complained about 'that tarnation Yankee rifle that they load on Sunday and shoot all week.' Those guns are also the reason Custer was defeated at Little Bighorn. Besides bows and arrows, the Lakota and Cheyenne warriors used Henry and Spencer repeating rifles against the single-shot Springfield Model 1873 carbines carried by the Federal cavalry troopers."

"I thought Custer was defeated because he was an arrogant fool."

Rod grinned. "That too, but going back to the Civil War, once Lincoln removed McClellan and put Grant as general-in-chief, things really starting humming for the North. Grant was relentless in his pursuit of Lee."

Rod walked me around the encampment, introducing me to his colleagues and explaining the uniforms and equipment. My previous belief that reenactments were a bunch of men playing "pretend soldier" and drinking beer for the weekend was pushed aside. I felt the blood rush to my face. Obviously, I was embarrassed by my lack of knowledge. It was all very interesting, but finally, I begged off. My leg was aching and it was late. "I've got to go, Rod. I'll see you tomorrow."

"Come early. It should be packed."

"I promise."

"Josiah?"

"Yeah."

"Thanks for taking an interest."

"You bet. We're buddies, aren't we?"

"For sure."

"I'll be here early. I promise."

Rod nodded and went back to putting up his pup tent.

I spied Franklin and Eunice walking toward the parking area and called out to them. "Hey, guys, wait for me. I'll just be a moment."

Eunice yelled back. "Don't be too long. You need to help me make the canapés. We have to get back."

"Just give me a minute." I hurried through the cars and trucks parked for the event, finally coming to Rod's red pickup truck. It was unlocked. I searched the front seat and glove compartment. Nothing unusual. Then I searched around the tires and the bumpers. Nothing. Feeling I might be on a wild goose chase I lowered my fingers, searching behind the car license plate in the back. Bingo!

I pulled out a small, magnetic GPS tracker. Well. Well. Looky here.

I didn't want to tell Rod about it as I believed he would confront the Statler brothers over it. I would tell him later. I put the tracker back as I knew Rod's truck wouldn't be moved for the next twenty-four hours. Why give the Statler brothers a heads-up that their tracking device had been discovered? I would remove it tomorrow and give it to Rod for the police.

Surely, the police would add it to the already existing charges.

Boy, was I naive or what!

5

Eunice and I, along with some other employees, worked late into the night to get the food ready for June's party. I had catered June's affairs for the past several years, so Bess and the rest of the DuPuy family could attend.

She drew up a list of foods readily accessible in 1865 for the menu. We made a mutton stew served with cornbread topped with freshly churned white butter, rhubarb/strawberry tarts, spicy pumpkin cakes, currant tarts with a sugar glaze, miniature apple fritters, watermelon wedges, and various dried fruit served with fruit wines, lemon water, and coffee.

As the staff was cleaning up, I slipped out and went to the Big House, where I spied a light on in Charles' office off the kitchen. The back door was open, so I let myself in and knocked on the office door.

"Come in."

I went inside the office. "Hey, Charles. You know you should really lock that kitchen door. I just walked in. It could have been anyone."

"Don't worry. I knew you were coming." Charles pointed to several monitors.

"Glad to see you installed some new security."

"I know you didn't come this late at night to discuss the door being unlocked. Is there a problem with the catering?"

"No. No. Everything is fine. I just wanted to ask if you remembered a Jimmy Ray Statler."

Charles rested his chin on his hand, musing, "Jimmy Ray Statler. Jimmy Ray Statler. That name is from a long time ago. I had only been working here for a year when Miss June fired Statler for stealing."

"Was he?"

"She wouldn't have fired him without cause, but I wasn't personally involved. Miss June had a farm manager at that time by the name of Rod Hiller. He's the one that brought the matter to Miss June's attention and actually fired Statler."

I was stunned. "That old bat. She didn't tell me."

"Excuse me?"

"Nothing. Is June still awake?"

"She has retired for the evening, Josiah. She's feeling poorly and needs her strength for tomorrow. Is there something I can help you with?"

I shook my head. "No, nothing, Charles. My people will be here with the food at seven sharp. Everything is ready to go. Sharlene will be in charge."

"I met her today. She came by to go over the details. I take it Miss Eunice is coming as a guest tomorrow night."

"As will I. What kind of party is this, Charles—a Civil War ball or a Halloween party? The invitation said to dress up in Civil War Attire."

"I think it is both. It's officially called a Remembrance Ball, but with strong tones of being a Halloween costume party." Charles waited for me to say something.

"Since we are supposed to attend in costume, are you coming as anyone in particular?"

Charles beamed a smile. "I'm coming as Ulysses S. Grant. I've always admired the man. What about you?"

"I bought one of those nineteenth-century dresses with crinolines. I even have the pantaloons, but I hate costume parties."

"It is near Halloween. Be a good sport and dress up. It's going to be fun."

"How many do you think are coming as John Wilkes Booth?"

"I hope no one. It would be as tasteless as someone dressing up as Lee Harvey Oswald."

Changing the subject, I said, "By the way, congratulations on your inheritance. Bess told me about your windfall."

"I owe it all to you, Jo. You talked Miss June into making us beneficiaries."

"June would have eventually come to the same conclusion. Your family has faithfully served her for many years. In fact, you are her family. Once she disinherited Lord Elsmere's nephew, the path was cleared for you."

"Still, it is a big thing and I thank you."

"It couldn't have happened to a nicer man." I looked at my watch. "I've got to get back and help Eunice tidy up. See you tomorrow, Charles."

He stood and walked me out the door to the back lawn. "Take a golf cart. It's too dark to walk home."

I waved and jumped into a cart left by the veranda. I sped past the corn maze that June had planted for the party. Guests and their children would enjoy traipsing inside it. Since it was so close to Halloween, jack-o-lanterns, straw bales, and scarecrows abounded. I wondered if June had other surprises waiting inside the corn maze. I certainly didn't want anyone jumping out at me if I went in.

I was too old for such frivolity.

But who doesn't like a scary corn maze around Halloween?

6

I got up early and was at the reenactment field before ten. The campsite was bustling with photographers and news station crews mingling among the history enthusiasts, neighing horses, barking dogs, and crying babies. Paramedics set up a first-aid station alongside an ambulance and a fire engine. People lined up at the porta-potties, volunteers poured water on camp fires, and soldiers practiced last minute drills before the battle. People like me dragged lawn chairs to vantage points where we could witness the battle.

A pathway had been mowed through the fields for the spectators to follow. Posted along the way, 20 x 24 photographs of generals, spies, abolitionists, politicians, and battle scenes with placards explaining their part in the Civil War, gave visitors a greater understanding of the period. I learned a few things myself.

Making my way through the Union campsite, I heard my name called. I turned to see Rod making his way toward me with his musket. I waited for him.

"I can't go into battle without a favor from a lady," Rod grinned. "Will you do me the honor?"

"Of course," I said, smiling. I took off my yellow scarf and tied it around his neck. "There you go." Since Rod's wife had died, I had taken him under my wing, so to speak. Nothing much. Just kept an eye out for him. Made sure he took his medications and kept his doctor appointments. Stuff like that.

I stood back and admired Rod.

He was dressed in a dashing blue wool uniform with silver buttons, polished black boots, and an authentic officer saber swung around his hip.

I said, "Don't fall on that thing. You'll break a hip."

"Noted."

"Are you going to ride a horse?"

"Naw, I'm with the infantry."

"Yeah, but you're a Captain. Don't you lead your men into battle on a horse?"

"Only the more experienced horsemen are to ride today since the cannons spook the horses. We've had several broken bones from soldiers falling off their steeds in the past. Horses have to be trained for the noise. They are in short supply currently."

I pulled my earplugs from my pocket and showed Rod. "I came prepared. Those cannons are too loud for my tender ears."

Rod nodded in agreement.

I needed to talk to Rod about the GPS device on his

truck, but wanted to ease into the topic. "You're wearing a different hat from yesterday."

"That was a kepi. This is a Hardee hat, nicknamed the Jeff Davis hat."

"That's ironic."

"The blue cord signifies the infantry and is always pinned up on the left side."

"I just keep learning more and more." I paused and looked around. "Rod, I need to talk to you about something. It's rather important."

"It's going to have to wait, Jo. I've got to gather my men together. The battle will start soon. Can your news wait?"

Darn. Darn. Darn. "Sure. Just one more thing—you look mighty handsome in that uniform, Rod. Honoria would be proud," I said, speaking of his late wife.

"Thank you, Jo. She always liked to come to these reenactments. This is my twentieth one."

"No kidding."

"I started out as a private."

"You told me."

"This is my last battle. I'm getting too old for it."

"You're a year younger than me, Rod."

"I feel old, Jo. I feel like I'm spread too thin in my mind. Know what I mean? Honoria's death took the stuffing out of me."

There was no denying what he said was true. When Rod and I had first met, we were both young, fit, and attractive. Now we were held together with spit and glue. Life had just beaten us up.

"Shucks, Rod, you're depressing me. I'm not ready for the grave and neither are you. You'll feel better after you knock someone on his butt today." I paused for a moment. "The Union Army did win this battle, didn't they?"

Looking sheepish, Rod said, "It was more of a draw. The Rebs knocked some of us on our butts as well. After all, this was a skirmish. The real battles were in Richmond and Perryville."

"Oh, well," I said. "Go have fun then. See you tonight at the ball, but tonight I need to speak with you about an important matter."

I don't think Rod was paying attention because he said absent-mindedly, "Lady Elsmere's group is on that hillside."

I looked to where he was pointing. "I see them. Thanks."

Rod tipped his blue Hardee hat and went to join his comrades.

I judged the distance up the hill, but didn't think I could make it. I had only so much energy to expend in a day and walking around was using up my reserves. To my surprise, a golf cart driven by Charles headed my way. I stood in place and waited.

"Need a ride?" Charles cheerfully asked.

"You bet." I thankfully climbed in.

"Who were you talking with?"

"Rod Hiller."

"I thought so. I haven't seen him in years. And we were just talking about him last night."

"Yes, we were."

When Charles sensed I didn't want to talk about Rod Hiller, he spoke of the evening's Remembrance Ball and how he was looking forward to it. Charles was going to give a speech about unity in a divided world.

Good luck with that, Charles, I thought to myself.

We reached the summit of the ridge where we would have a splendid view of the battle. A canopy was ready with tables jam-packed with food and drink. All of Charles' family was present as was Eunice.

"Kind of reminds one of the First Battle of Bull Run in 1861 when the citizens of Washington D. C. rode out in carriages and brought picnic baskets to watch the battle, only to flee when it turned out to be a very bloody day. Over five thousand dead and wounded," Eunice noted.

Bess said, "I guess the spectators vamoosed after they realized those men were fighting for their lives with real guns and not play acting."

I recounted, "It is now estimated that approximately 600,000 to 750,000 soldiers from both sides died fighting this war. That doesn't include civilians killed, soldiers maimed for life, property destroyed or confiscated, towns burned to the ground, wildlife and livestock slaughtered, Lincoln assassinated—the list goes on and on. The total population at that time was only thirty-one million."

"A terrible cost for terrible sins," Charles murmured.

I took a deep sigh. Americans must never, never let ourselves get this close to civil war again, no matter what.

Charles set up my lawn chair for me, although there was plenty of seating. Shaneika, Eunice's daughter and my criminal lawyer, showed up. Her son, Lincoln, and Shaneika's date, Mike Connor, June's farm manager, also joined us.

I knew Shaneika Mary Todd would be here as she was a history buff. In her office is a Confederate officer's saber, a letter to Mary Todd's brother from Abraham Lincoln, and a daguerreotype of African American women on wash day at Camp Nelson. When I asked Shaneika about her collection, she merely replied they were family heirlooms. And as much as I poked and pried, I could never get Shaneika to tell me how she is related to Mary Todd Lincoln's family.

Lincoln came over and sat on the ground beside me, looking behind my chair. "Where's Baby?"

"I left him at home. The noise would have frightened him. No need to put Baby through that."

The youngster looked down the hill to where the Union soldiers were gathering.

"So the North started the war?"

"No, it was the South. Fort Sumter was fired upon, but the war was going to happen regardless. A perfect storm was forming."

"All Northerners thought slavery was a sin?"

"Not all, but enough of them."

"All Southerners believed slavery was right?"

"Not all, but enough of them."

"I'm glad I don't live in those times."

I laughed. "I am too, Linc. I am, too."

"We studied the Civil War, but all those battles and which general fought on which side is hard to remember—it's so confusing."

I wanted to keep it simple for Lincoln. He would learn of the complexities of this war as he took more advanced courses. There was no point in telling this little boy that we were still wrestling with the same prejudices as during that time period. Let him keep his childhood as long as possible. Recounting Rod's conversation, I said, "It's important that we know our history—the good and the bad. The Civil War was a terrible event, but we healed as a nation. E Pluribus Unum."

"Huh? What does that mean?"

"Out of many—one. It's our country's motto. Something we should all remember. Be sure to take Latin in school, Linc. It will serve you well."

"Be quiet," Shaneika said, shushing us both. "Lady

Elsmere is about to speak."

Linc and I turned our attention to a black and gold gilded carriage drawn by two black horses in the meadow where June stood holding a large purple ribbon banner. Charles' daughter, Amelia, stood by June in the carriage to aid her. June looked regal wearing a mauve dress of the period, a lace shawl, white gloves, and some sort of frou-frou hat that looked like a bird had landed on her head. Somehow the costume worked together.

"What's she saying? I can't hear a word." Of course, I couldn't because I had taken off my hearing aid. Bad move on my part. I heard a mumbling coming from the microphone, Lady Elsmere dropping the purple banner, and cheering from the crowd. I wondered if purple had any significance.

The Union Drum Corp began striking their eagle drums as the Union soldiers took their positions.

I have to be completely honest. I didn't think I was going to like the reenactment, but the scene forming below us was compelling. The Union infantry soldiers lined up and began marching toward their opponents not yet seen. Quarter Horses carrying handsome officers pranced in front of the columns while bugles, drums, and fifes played *The Battle Hymn of the Republic* as Union soldiers sang the lyrics.

I sang along as well.

Mine eyes have seen the glory of the coming of the Lord. He is trampling out the vintage where the grapes of wrath are stored. He has loosed the fateful lightning of his terrible swift sword. His truth is marching on. Glory, glory hallelujah. Glory, glory hallelujah. Glory, glory hallelujah. His truth is marching on.

From the ridge to my right, I could hear a different wave of sound—the crunching of hundreds of soldiers marching in step.

Fumbling in my pants pocket, I pulled out my hearing aid. I was missing too much of the action with the sound cut off. I hurriedly put it on.

Just as I did, the Johnny Rebs reached the top of the ridge with Confederate flags gaily dancing in the breeze. A gray American Saddlebred horse led the troops. His rider was wearing a Confederate general's uniform. I immediately made the connection that the horse was supposed to represent Traveller, Robert E. Lee's horse, and the rider—the Confederate general himself. Not historically accurate to Kentucky, but rather stirring to witness. The real Traveller outlived Lee and followed the General's coffin with Lee's boots backward in the stirrups. Only a year later, Traveller stepped on a rusty nail and contracted lockjaw. He was euthanized and eventually interred at Lee Chapel in Lexington, Virginia. Not a very glorious end for such a noble animal.

Suddenly, the Johnny Rebs cried in unison the famous bloodcurdling rebel yell, which put fear in many a man's heart, before they started advancing rapidly down the hill.

The Confederate artillery immediately rolled small cannons into place on top of the small ridge and began bombarding the Union troops now taking cover behind fallen logs, rock walls, and trees. As the Union troops were lower than the Confederates, who were mainly on the east slope of the steep hillside, the men in blue seemed to be at quite a disadvantage.

The blasts from the cannons were so loud, I removed my hearing aid and put my earplugs back in. I could feel as well as hear the reports from the cannons. Linc covered his ears with his hands, but his face glowed with anticipation and excitement.

We had gone from singing to shooting, cannons volleying, horses screaming, men shouting in a matter of seconds. The Union colonel, on the Quarter Horse, jumped off and slapped the rump of his mare, which happily galloped in the opposite direction. Brandishing his sword in the air and beckoning his men to follow, the officer bellowed, "CHARGE!"

Charge they did through the meadow to meet the oncoming Confederates. The noise was deafening, and the acrid smoke of the cannons rode on the breeze.

I brought up my binoculars to find Rod keeping up with the younger men rushing forth in the front line. Suddenly he fell on one knee, but raised up enough to shoot his musket. Recovering quickly, he reloaded and leaned on his gun to get up and rushed forward.

Tugging on my sleeve, Linc asked if he could use

my binoculars. I gave them to him, having no problem following my yellow scarf in the battle now that I had spotted Rod.

Out of the corner of my eye, I saw two Confederate soldiers break rank and rush past the Confederate general into no-mans-land between the two fighting armies, and then past Union officers leading the Federal troops.

"What are those two men doing?" I asked our group. I didn't expect anyone to answer. It was rather a rhetorical question.

The two Confederates headed for Rod where they raised their guns.

Rod stopped in surprise when confronted.

I learned from Rod that the reenactors had been given placards as to who was to do what and when, since this skirmish was rarely reenacted. This was a play after all, and everyone had been assigned their bit. The two Confederates fired their pistols and Rod fell.

I shot out of my seat. I knew that Rod was supposed to reach the top of the ridge before he was struck down. This was not part of his acting assignment.

The two assailants ran back up the hill to merge with their fellow Confederates.

"Linc, give me the binoculars." I grabbed the binoculars and watched the two soldiers go in the opposite direction of their fellow soldiers and disappear over the ridge. "Charles, I think you better check on that soldier with the yellow scarf. He might be really hurt."

"It's part of the script," Charles said, looking to where I was pointing.

"I don't think so. I think that man was really attacked. It's Rod Hiller."

Looking concerned, Charles said, "Show me again."

"He's the one wearing a yellow scarf. I fear something is wrong."

"Look!" Charles said, pointing.

Several Union soldiers were bending over Rod until one waved a white flag to officials observing the battle. Seeing the white flag, the order was given to sound the siren, which meant all participants were to halt in place immediately.

Charles and I got into a golf cart and rushed to the meadow where an ambulance was now making its way across the field. We arrived at a little knot of soldiers surrounding Rod and pushed our way through.

"What has happened?" Charles asked.

One of the soldiers said, "Looks like someone was using live ammunition."

The ambulance pulled up and two paramedics jumped out, running past us. I still wasn't close enough to see Rod, but I listened to paramedics work.

June and Amelia pulled up in another golf cart close to us.

Amelia asked, "Dad, what's happened?"

Charles got out of the cart and spoke with June. I was too far away to hear what he said, but whatever he murmured to June caused her great distress. I could see it on her face as she motioned Amelia to drive away.

I got out of the cart and followed Charles through the small knot of men, which had grown larger with Confederate soldiers now joining. As I pushed my way through, I saw the paramedics treating Rod who was lying on the ground. I asked one of the soldiers, whom Rod had introduced to me as Saginaw, "What happened to Rod?"

"Some dang fool didn't check his gun and Rod got shot."

"Did you see who did it?"

"It was one of two men who rushed past us. They ran back up the hill."

That coincided with what I had witnessed. "Do you know who they were?"

"Looked like those boys from yesterday. They were dressed as privates, so they shouldn't be too hard to track down."

"I thought all the guns were checked before the battle."

"They are. Only powder is supposed to be used."

"Did you see the weapon? Was it a period weapon or a modern pistol?"

The man shook his head. "I couldn't tell you. Too much was going on, and it happened so fast."

Hearing clapping from the bystanders, I turned to see the paramedics help Rod stand. He had a large bandage wrapped around his head. Rod smiled and waved. "It takes more than a musket ball to keep me down, fellers."

Relief ran through the ranks, and there was much cheering as the paramedics placed Rod on a gurney. To my surprise, Charles jumped into the ambulance after Rod was eased in by paramedics.

Before the ambulance's doors closed, I yelled, "Rod, give me a call when you can."

Standing next to me, Saginaw said, "There goes one lucky SOB. An eighth of an inch closer and Rod would be a dead man. Almost seemed intentional, didn't it?"

"What do you mean?"

"Missing Rod at that short distance. He should have plugged him for sure."

Funny that Rod's friend should say that.

I was thinking the exact same thing.

7

June turned the dismal event around. Since the shooting needed to be investigated, the reenactment could not go forward as planned. June allowed the soldiers to drill to the amusement of onlookers for no one could leave until the police questioned everybody. The cavalry rode their horses about the fields, stopping to explain their equipment to small groups of sight-seers, who took pictures with the trained horses and riders. To further dull everyone's disappointment, June announced that the food trucks, stationed in the parking area, were open free of charge to all soldiers, volunteers, and spectators.

You better believe I stood in line. I had a yen for grease and salt. As I was getting a barbeque sandwich and lemonade from one of the trucks, Eunice found me.

"This is so terrible," Eunice complained. "All the work to put this event on, and some idiot didn't check his weapon."

"I don't think that is what happened."

"Oh?"

"I've talked with several of the old timers, and they swear all guns are checked by the officers right before the battle. That would tell me that a reenactor loaded live ammunition after his gun was checked."

"What are you saying, Josiah?"

"I'm saying we're looking at attempted murder, Eunice. Murder in front of hundreds of confused witnesses, who didn't understand what they were seeing until it was too late. Fortunately for Rod, the gun either misfired or the shooter was a terrible shot."

"Why do you think it was Rod who was the intended target and not just a random accident?"

"Because I saw who did it. It was the Statler brothers. They rushed from the Confederate side to the Union front line and shot almost point blank. Their target was Rod all along."

"But why?"

"That's what I intend to find out. It must have to do with more than some stolen agate."

Eunice looked thoughtful. "Well, start sleuthing tomorrow. Miss June is still having the ball tonight. She's having a pumpkin carving contest, trick and treating plus apple bobbing for the children—not to mention the dance for the grownups. I hope you have polished up on the quadrille. You'll be expected to participate."

"Not with my gimpy leg," I said emphatically, patting my left leg. "My dancing days are over."

Our attention turned to the local police, aided by the Civil War *officers*, now fanning out through the campgrounds. I could see them in the parking lot asking questions and inspecting guns in vehicles. My stomach clenched into a sour ball.

I turned my attention back to Eunice. "I'm going to the Butterfly and see if Sharlene needs help."

"She won't be there until six. We set up at the Big House at seven. The ball starts at eight. Since children are going to be there, I expect the ball to be over by eleven."

"Are you coming to the Butterfly?" I asked.

"No. I'll meet everyone at the Big House at seven, and I mean seven sharp. That means everything needs to be loaded up and moving by six-thirty."

"I'll make sure we're on time, Eunice, but I think I'll have a little talk with Miss June first. I think she has left out some details from her story."

"What story?"

"I'll tell you later." I motioned for Eunice to turn around as Shaneika and Linc were walking up to us. I didn't want Lincoln to behold any more shenanigans.

"Is that man dead?" Lincoln asked.

"He's on the mend, Linc. He's at the hospital where they'll make him right as rain."

"He looked dead," Linc commented.

"He was pretty convincing, that's for sure."

"What happened?" Shaneika asked me.

"Someone forgot to check their pistol for live ammunition. It happens," I said, shaking my head slightly to Shaneika. I didn't want to discuss this in front of Lincoln.

Shaneika took the hint and bribed Lincoln with an ice cream cone.

I went in search of Lady Elsmere, but she had gone back to the Big House, or so I was told by Charles, who whizzed by in his golf cart.

I was getting more frustrated by the moment. This was turning into a very bad day. I wondered how the rest of it would go.

8

Police combed the area with metal detectors, trying to find the bullet that struck Rod Hiller. It wasn't long before they found something. I wasn't close enough to either hear or see what they had found, but several gathered in a tiny cluster looking at something. Then I saw a forensic technician put a small object into an evidence bag. My thoughts were flashing like blinking cop lights, but a clear conclusion eluded my grasp. I couldn't grab hold of anything substantial, except that I didn't believe this morning's snafu to be an accident, but attempted murder.

Since the area was cordoned off, I decided to go to Rod's car and retrieve the tracking device, but first I needed a cop to go with me. "Excuse me. Excuse me, Officer. I have some information for you regarding the attack on Rod Hiller."

A young man wearing a navy suit and a crisp white shirt turned around. He looked vaguely familiar. "Mrs. Reynolds. We meet again."

I stared at this tall, dark-haired young man who looked energetic and full of promise. He almost quivered with vitality. "I'm sorry, but I have forgotten your name." The truth of the matter was I couldn't place him, but I knew we had met before. It was embarrassing that I couldn't remember him. My memory was not what it used to be. Isn't getting older grand?

He took off his sunglasses and gave me a limp handshake. "I am Jeremy Snow. I guarded your house one summer. You gave me vegetables."

I brightened. "Yes, you were in uniform. No wonder I couldn't place you. Out of context. You've been promoted, I see."

Snow smiled broadly. "Yes, ma'am. Working in Vice at the moment, but was called in for this case, but I'm afraid attempted homicide is not my forte."

"Give it time," I teased. "I take it that the police think Mr. Hiller's accident was no accident at all then. Since Mr. Hiller didn't die, shouldn't this be a violent crime case?"

"I was asked to help with the interviews, so here I am," Snow said. "When Lady Elsmere calls, we jump. This 'accident' will make the national papers because of her involvement, so we want to close this incident as fast as possible. Our chief doesn't want us to look like some backwater hicksville."

I thought Snow's remarks were very forthcoming

and most unwise. He would learn not to be so honest after he was quoted in the papers a few times. I just hoped no reporter was in hearing distance.

As an afterthought, Snow added, "I keep up with you in the papers."

"I seem to have a knack of getting my name in the media for all the wrong reasons."

"It seemed you were looking for someone. May I help you?"

"I was looking for an officer to talk about Rod Hiller."

Officer Snow looked blank. "Come again?"

"He's the guy that got shot today."

"What about him?"

"Take a walk with me and I'll show you." I gave Snow a brief rundown of what had transpired between Rod and the Statler brothers, while we walked over to the pickup truck. We were surprised to find two men, still in their Civil War duds, leaning on the vehicle looking perplexed.

"Hello gentlemen. Is there a problem?" Officer Snow asked.

I recognized Saginaw. He was popping up everywhere today.

Rod's friend tipped his kepi hat. "Ma'am. Officer."

"Something wrong, Saginaw? You look frustrated," I commented.

"Rod is being released from the hospital. It apparently was just a graze. He called and wants us to pack up his gear and drive his truck to the hospital. When we got here, the tires were slashed. The truck's gonna have to be towed into town now."

I took out my phone. "I'll call Lady Elsmere's people. She had mechanics working today. They can tow the truck over to the farm shop, and someone can run into town and get new tires."

As I was talking with the head mechanic on my phone, Officer Snow asked the gentlemen if Rod was having trouble with anyone.

"He sure was," Saginaw said, unbuttoning his heavy and scratchy infantry uniform. "I took this yesterday when two fellows tried to start something with Rod." He pulled out a phone from his pocket and showed Snow.

Snow played the video several times before handing the phone back. "Do you know who they are?"

I peered at the video. "They are Curry and Skeeter Statler, the men I was telling you about. I witnessed this happening myself."

Snow nodded and jotted in a notebook. Glancing up at us, he said, "I'd like to have a look inside the vehicle before it is towed away."

The two men gathered around while Snow opened the truck and searched inside.

"How do you happen to have the key to this truck?" Snow asked.

Saginaw offered, "There are several participants who don't have family here to hold onto their keys for safekeeping, so we give them to our commanding officer to keep in a box in his tent. We went by, picked up the keys, and came right over to the truck."

Rod's other friend, dressed in a Confederate sergeant's uniform, added, "Too many of us have lost our keys in fields doing drills or during a battle. This way we know our keys are safe."

Snow asked, "Is this box locked?"

The sergeant scratched his chin. "We just went into the tent and got the keys."

Saginaw said, "The box is tucked away. Very few people know it exists. The Confederate commanding officer does the same for his people."

"What that really means is everyone knows vehicle and house keys are kept in unsecure boxes inside officer tents." Snow shook his head.

Saginaw said, "Well, if you put it that way."

His friend piped up, "But the general public doesn't know. Why do you ask?"

Snow held out a modern .22 revolver. "Because I found this in Mr. Hiller's glove compartment and it has been fired recently."

Ooooops!

9

The three of us stared at the revolver in Snow's gloved hand and then at each other.

Snow asked, "Was the truck locked when you tried to open it?"

Saginaw answered, "Yes, sir."

"Is this Rod Hiller's gun?"

Both men looked glumly at the gun. "We've never seen it before."

"So this is not the gun that shot Mr. Hiller?"

"We can't say. It happened so fast. We were behind Rod, and these two Johnny Rebs rushed him with both of them shooting. He went down."

"What happened then?"

"I bent down to help Rod stand up because I knew he was scripted to die at the top of the hill, but he was unconscious. Then I saw the blood. I threw up a white flag that denotes 'man down.' We only do that if it is serious. The siren sounded and the battle stopped."

The other man whistled before stating, "We don't

know what happened to those two guys who charged Rod, but I do know they were privates. They weren't part of our regular crew."

Snow asked, "Were they the same men who had words with Rod Hiller yesterday?"

The Confederate sergeant said, "I was on the ridge when Rod got shot. Didn't see it happen. There was a lot going on."

"It could be them. Their hats were pulled down, so I can't swear for sure," Saginaw said, wiping sweat off his face with a dirty bandana.

Snow tried to make sense of the event. "Let me get this right. Every man knows his role in the reenactment?"

"Just in this skirmish. We had never reenacted it before, so everyone was given a part to play based on the military records we had. In most reenactments, the officers direct the battle."

"I see." Snow turned to me. "Recognize this gun?"

I replied, "Never seen it before. Do you think it's the gun used on Rod?"

Snow sniffed the barrel. "Ballistics will have to confirm but if it is, how did the gun wind up in Mr. Hiller's glove compartment? These gentlemen said the truck was locked."

"Like you said, the truck keys were in a box where anyone could have stolen them and then put the keys back."

Snow asked, "Why would they need the keys if the truck was unlocked? You said the truck was open yesterday."

I didn't have an answer. "The Statler boys had been harassing him. I mean Rod didn't cut his own tires. Look at the slashes on the rubber. They weren't there yesterday when I checked the truck and no gun was in the glove compartment. I checked the entire truck. That's how I came across the GPS device. That gun was not in Rod's truck."

"Did you lock the truck?"

I was emphatic. "NO!"

"Maybe without thinking about it?"

"No. I'm sure."

"Who put the gun in the truck and locked it?" Snow mumbled to himself, jotting in his notebook. Afterward, he made Rod's friends wrote down their names and contact information.

"What are we going to do about Rod?" Saginaw asked. "He's expecting us."

I said, "I'll have Lady Elsmere take care of it. She'll have someone pick Rod up from the hospital and invite him to stay with her at the Big House for a few days."

Saginaw said, "That would be good because Rod's got nobody to help him at home."

The Confederate soldier asked sheepishly, "Is the party still on?"

I replied, "I think so. Make sure you both come.

Rod will need his friends. Seeing you both will give him a boost."

Both men looked happier. The weekend would not be a total loss. "Okay then. Officer, are you finished with us?"

"For now. Thank you."

"Sure. Anytime."

As soon as the men were out of earshot, Snow asked, "Now show me where you found the GPS tracker."

"It was behind the license plate."

Snow went around the vehicle with me following close behind. He stuck his hand behind the plate and felt around. The tracker wasn't there.

I protested, "I swear I put that tracker back."

"It's not here now."

Both Snow and I scoured the grass. We came up empty handed.

"What do you think?" I asked.

"I think Mr. Hiller's got some explaining to do. Based on his answers, he might have a real problem."

"I don't understand."

"Mr. Hiller could have two men after him who wish him harm."

"I hear an 'or.'"

"He could have set this up himself."

I said, "How could Rod have shot himself? You talked to multiple witnesses who said they saw two men rush up, point two guns at him and fire. Rod was injured."

Snow took out a handkerchief and wiped the corners of his mouth. He folded the hanky neatly and put it back in his pocket.

"The whole story sounds fishy."

"I witnessed it myself. That's what happened."

"Two men rush Mr. Hiller and shoot at him. Hiller gets grazed by one bullet. His attackers must have been really lousy shots. If they were as close as you say they were, why isn't Mr. Hiller lying in the morgue?"

"I don't know."

"And where is the other bullet? If both men were pointing guns at Mr. Hiller, it makes sense that they both had guns with live ammunition. Our men have gone over that field and have found a modern .22 bullet—not a musket ball. I think that bullet came from this gun, which will lead us to conclude only one of the guns had live ammunition. If they truly wanted to kill Mr. Hiller, wouldn't both of them have fired live rounds? The story doesn't make sense."

"You've only been looking less than an hour. Perhaps the bullet from the other gun has been overlooked. It's a big field."

"If the other gun had live ammunition and didn't strike Hiller, why didn't it strike anyone else? Now, if it had been me and I wanted to kill a man, I certainly wouldn't use a .22 revolver. I'd use something with more of a punch. And another thing—why make such a spectacle in front of everyone? Why not load a musket with a Minié ball and shoot Hiller during the battle? Then claim it was an accident."

I was smoldering with indignation, but Snow was right. The entire shooting was too theatrical, but I pressed on. "How can you explain the slashed tires, the planted gun in Rod's car, and the missing GPS tracker?"

"First of all, you are Mr. Hiller's friend, so your testimony that you found a GPS tracker is suspect."

"Second?"

"Like I said, Mr. Hiller could have set this up himself."

"For what purpose?"

"Your guess is as good as mine."

"I'm telling you the Statler brothers are setting Rod up for a fall."

"We shall see, Mrs. Reynolds. I'm going to have the truck impounded until we get to the bottom of this."

"That truck is Rod's only means of transportation."

"Since this happened on Lady Elsmere's land, I suggest she give Mr. Hiller a loaner car."

"This stinks. Rod is the victim here. I hate hearing that you suspect him of something nefarious." I was furious. "Are you going to track down the Statler brothers?"

"We'll see them and get their version."

"And?"

Snow pulled sunglasses from his jacket and put them on. "We'll have a conversation with them and see what they say."

"It's a shame this incident has blighted the reenactment. All the work that was put into it was for nothing."

Snow glanced around at the spectators finally being allowed to leave. "Mrs. Reynolds, I think people are having a good time. They'll have a wild story to share at church tomorrow. Look at them."

I did indeed see smiling visitors strolling to their cars in a leisurely manner, chatting excitedly, and taking last minute pictures. However, I felt like potato salad left out at a Fourth of July picnic.

Charles drove over in his golf cart with the tow truck following behind while spewing diesel fumes.

Snow waved him off. Confused that Snow didn't want the farm's tow truck, Charles got out of his golf cart. The two chewed the fat for a moment or two before Snow beckoned a uniformed cop to watch the truck.

Things were not looking good for Rod.

Or was someone trying to sabotage Lady Elsmere, and Rod just got caught up in it?

I had a bad feeling about the party tonight.

A real bad feeling.

10

I ran to the front door and opened it, fussing, "It's about time."

"Relax, Miss Pittypat. There's plenty of time," Franklin said. He turned, showing off his Confederate uniform. "What do you think?"

"I think my ancestor tried to kill your ancestor and vice versa."

"I'll have you know this uniform is authentic. Look at it. Not one moth hole. Been preserved with care. You know whose uniform this is?"

"I know all about your family. I'm dating your brother. Remember?"

"How is dear old Hunter?"

"He called last night. He's coming home next week for a rest before he heads out again."

"Hunter works too hard. I've told him we should sell Wickliffe, but he wants to save it. For what reason, I ask? It's not like either one of us have children to carry on the Wickliffe legacy," Franklin said. "It's a money pit."

"I thought most of the debt was paid off."

"It is."

I turned my back to Franklin. "Can you hook me up?"

Franklin gave me the once-over. "I thought you were going to wear the black gown."

"Eunice and I traded. She decided she didn't like the blue one after all. Now hook me up."

Franklin examined the dress. "How many petticoats have you got underneath the skirt?"

"Enough. Come on, Franklin. We're going to be late. I want to see Lady Elsmere's grand entrance."

"Aren't you the same woman from yesterday complaining about this ball—saying we shouldn't be dragging up the painful past?"

"I want to have some fun. Please hook me up. You promised you would help me with this dress."

"Okay, be still."

I shivered.

"What's the matter?"

I said, "Your hands are cold."

"You know what they say. Cold hands, warm heart. There. You're hooked up and ready to party."

I lifted my skirts and hustled to my bedroom to look in the full length mirror. I did look rather pretty. I am not a beautiful woman. Attractive is all I would say about my looks, but I felt beautiful in this gown. I swayed this way and that, playing with the bounce of the skirt. This ball gown was something I could wear for an hour or two, but I couldn't see how women wore such a contraption every day. The dress was constrictive and heavy. No wonder women fainted all the time back then. They couldn't breathe because they couldn't expand their lungs when they got agitated.

Franklin lazily leaned against the bedroom door jamb. "Yeah. Yeah. Come on, Josiah. We're going to be late."

"I thought you said we had plenty of time."

"This was if we were discussing my costume—not yours."

We both heard the front door open.

Franklin looked at me curiously. "Expecting any-one?"

Since Baby didn't react, I called out, "Hello?"

A woman called out, "It's me, Josiah. We forgot a few things."

Both Franklin and I went into the great room where Sharlene was raiding the walk-in freezer. She pulled out two baskets.

"Everything okay?" I asked.

Sharlene turned toward me, smiling. "Oh, sure. I forgot the jams for the scones. Eunice is already at the Big House and we've set up. Everything's good to go." She looked at her watch. "Gotta get moving. Guests will begin arriving soon."

I sighed with relief. "We'll be leaving now. Can you lock up?"

"Sure. No problem. You two go on. I'll be following in a moment. I'm looking for an apricot puree I made this morning."

Franklin crooked his arm. "Shall we, my lady?"

I took hold of his arm and we moved toward the front door until I heard a thump thump behind me. It was Baby thinking he was coming, too. "No, Baby. You're staying home. I'll only be gone for a couple of hours."

I swear that dog looked hurt. I yelled, "Sharlene, call Baby for a treat. He'll come to you."

Sharlene called from the kitchen. "Baby. Baby. Treat. Treat."

Baby gave me one last baleful look before he trotted for the kitchen.

As soon as he turned the corner, Franklin and I made haste out the front door. We tried his Smart car, but I couldn't fit in it with my voluminous skirts, so we took my golf cart, parking in the back by the Big House's kitchen. I wanted to see how my catering staff was doing and slipped in the back door while Franklin went around to the front door. He wanted to make a grand entrance.

Even though I wasn't wearing a hoop, I still had to turn sideways to fit through the door, but I finally made it. My staff was busily filling up champagne flutes placed on trays. "Everything okay?"

One of the waiters nodded, "We're doing fine. Did

you see Sharlene?"

"Yes. She'll be here very soon."

"That's good. We need to put the jams out and then we are finished."

"Eunice around?"

"She's checking the buffet."

"Thanks." Realizing that I was in the way, I hurried into the grand foyer and found Eunice messing with flower arrangements. "May I help?"

"It's this darn dress," Eunice said of her black mourning gown. "I can't get close enough to pull out that flower sticking out."

The doorbell rang.

Eunice looked at me with panic. "My goodness, they're early."

"It's just Franklin."

"Ah jeez, gave me quite a start."

"It's still a half hour until guests arrive."

One of our staff assigned to handle the front entrance opened the door to Franklin, who strode in as though he had won the Civil War single-handedly. I'm surprised he didn't come in on a horse.

"There's no one here to see you, Franklin," I said.

Franklin looked disappointed. "I'll just have to 'arrive' again when more people are here."

Eunice asked, "Franklin, can you pull that gladiolus out for me? You're a tall person."

Franklin reached up and pulled out the distracting

perennial. "Here you go."

"Thanks."

Franklin looked at the buffet. "May I partake of something?"

"Don't you dare touch that food, Franklin Wickliffe. It's for the guests."

"What am I? Chopped liver?"

I pushed Franklin toward the elevator. "Let's go torment Lady Elsmere. You can play with her jewelry."

Franklin got that sloppy grin on his face when we do something he likes. "Good idea."

We both rode the elevator. I wish June would get it fixed. It groaned and shimmied. It didn't inspire confidence, but it takes me too long to climb the stairs.

I knocked on June's door. "June. It's Franklin and me. May we come in? We want to see your dress."

"Entrez-vous."

Amelia opened the locked door.

"Why's the door locked?" I asked.

"To keep people like you from barging in."

"Noted." I gave Amelia a hangdog look.

"Come in since you're here."

Franklin pushed by both of us and flung himself in a chair. "My gawd, June. You look gorgeous!"

I poked my head around Amelia and gasped. June did look gorgeous. She was wearing a high collared, blue fleur-de-lis brocade dress crisscrossed with silver trimming and accented by white gloves. She wore simple pearl earrings and her styled white hair boasted a pearl diadem of the period. June looked beyond elegant. She looked regal.

"Who made the dress?" I asked, fingering the material.

"Amelia copied it from a picture of one of Lord Elsmere's ancestors."

"I had no idea you were such a seamstress, Amelia," I said. "Congratulations."

Amelia said, "I had lots of help from a professional. I just supervised after I hired a wonderful seamstress from Versailles. She's really a quilt maker, but said she'd try her hand at sewing this dress. I think she did a wonderful job."

"She did. My goodness, I don't think I've seen such a beautiful period dress, except in a museum." I glumly glanced down at my off-the-rack costume. "I feel like the ginger-haired step-daughter at the ball now."

"Will this help?" June held out a splendid diamond choker.

I almost leapt for it as I wanted to wear it so much, but I held back. "You can't make a silk purse out of a sow's ear. I'll do with what I've got on."

Franklin jumped up. "I'll wear it."

I pushed Franklin back in his seat. "Shut up and behave."

Franklin groused, "Takes the fun out of living."

June gave the choker to Amelia to put away in the

vault. "I'm afraid Josiah's right. We must be historically correct. Confederate officers did not wear diamond chokers to dances."

"I think I hear the first guests arriving," Amelia said, opening the bedroom door a little. She closed and locked it again.

"How are you going to stuff that hooped dress in a wheelchair?" I asked.

"I'm not using my wheelchair. Charles and Rodney are escorting me down the staircase."

"Do you think you can negotiate the staircase in that dress?" I shot a look at Amelia, who pursed her lips in disagreement with the plan.

"I think I'll be all right, Josiah. You worry too much."

"Rod was grazed by a bullet today. I don't think he's the best candidate to escort anyone down a marble staircase. There's a probability he might become dizzy."

"Tosh," June said.

"What do you think, Amelia?" I asked, hoping she would back me up.

"I've told Miss June she should go down the elevator, but she won't listen to me. I think what she is planning to do is folly."

"There—you have it."

"Oh, shut up, Josiah. This may be my last ball. I want to make a grand gesture. If I go out, I want to go out on my feet."

Franklin cracked, "It may indeed be your last grand gesture if you fall, but you'll be taking Rod and Charles with you."

"I've made up my mind. Now will you both go downstairs and leave me in peace."

"June?"

"Go please. You're spoiling my big night," June said, looking upset.

Amelia beckoned us to leave.

I didn't mean to upset June, but I did mean to speak with Rod. "What room is Rod in?"

Amelia whispered, "Last room on the right."

"How does he seem?"

"I haven't seen him. My son picked him up at the hospital and said he acted fine. Since Mr. Hiller's been here, he's been in his room resting."

"I see."

"Jo, go on now. I'll see to Miss June. All we have to do is get her down those stairs in one piece. Daddy is aware of the challenge. I'll speak with Mr. Hiller and make sure he's fit to see June down the stairs. You can talk to him later at the ball."

"Okay. I'll see you in a few. By the way, your dress is outstanding as well."

Amelia smoothed down the off-the-shoulder, red taffeta dress with balloon sleeves. "The same lady made it for me. Red's my favorite color."

Franklin added, "It is a stunning dress, Miss Amelia."

"Thank you. You two go on. I'll take care of things here."

Franklin and I scooted into the elevator, sending us to the first floor. A great many guests had arrived, and the hired band began to play songs from the Civil War era. Noisy children were escorted outside for games, pumpkin carving, and trick or treating in the corn maze where there were candy stations. Each child was given a small burlap sack for their candy.

I spied Eunice and Shaneika standing in a corner observing the crowd. Franklin and I went over to them. "How's it going, Eunice?"

"Smoothly. Very smoothly."

"Need me for anything?"

"Naw, you'll just get in the way."

"Loved to be needed." I turned to Shaneika wearing a strapless black dress with a lot of white tulle under the knee length black skirt. "The invitation said all comers must wear a costume, so where's yours?"

"I'm not wearing one of those antebellum dresses on principle."

"I thought you would jump at the chance since you are such a Civil War buff."

"Doesn't mean I want to dress up in corsets and hoops."

"You look like you're going to your senior prom."

"It was my senior prom dress," Shaneika replied, smug that she had not gained weight since high school.

She didn't need to add that both Eunice and I had put on a few pounds since we were eighteen.

I pushed aside her comment and asked, "Linc here?"

"He's outside with the rest of the children."

Eunice added, "The candy stations have only the type of treats that would have been available during the Civil War—rock sugar candy, Horehound candy, Necco Wafers, jelly beans, peppermint sticks, taffy, peanuts, apples, and sugared nuts."

"No chocolate?" Franklin asked astounded. "Horehound candy sounds disgusting."

Amused, Eunice tilted her head. "Sorry, Franklin, but it's not bad. You should try it."

"I'll beg off. I see the dancing has started and a lady is in need of a partner. I'm off. Catch up with you all later." Franklin grabbed two flutes of champagne before rushing off.

"What's up with Franklin?"

"Nothing. He's excited because he's wearing some ancestor's uniform. He thinks he's the belle of the ball."

Eunice snapped her fingers. "That's why Franklin smelled of mothballs." We both grinned at each other until Eunice's eyes widened and her smile dropped off her face.

"Anything wrong?" I asked, grabbing her arm.

"The party just went south. Take a look."

I turned to see Curry and Skeeter Statler enter the grand foyer. Curry was wearing a Union lieutenant's uniform while Skeeter sported a Confederate lieutenant's uniform.

We weren't the only ones who noticed them. Men stopped dancing only to stare at the two men approaching the buffet table. There was a low murmur of discontent throughout the foyer.

"What's happening?"

"I think the news of Rod's attack has spread throughout the reenactors, but I believe the main reason is the Statler brothers are wearing lieutenant uniforms. They are not entitled to wear them. They are privates."

"Other guests are wearing officer uniforms. Franklin is."

"But they are not reenactors. These people have very strict rules of conduct for their own."

Saginaw and others approached the brothers and surrounded them.

Eunice asked, "What should we do? They're near the food."

"We get paid regardless. Let them duke it out."

"You mean a fight? No. No. No. Our company worked too hard on researching, cooking, and setting up that buffet table. It's not easy to serve nineteenth-century fare in our modern era. I'm not gonna let some cracker tear up my beautiful display."

"Your prejudices are showing, Eunice. And your crinoline is too, by the way."

"This is not the time for jokes, Josiah."

"Go over and stop it then."

"How?"

"You're a woman. Charm them."

"Josiah?" Eunice gave me a pleading look.

"All right. I'll come with you." We started across the room toward the men as comrades arm-in-arm.

Sure enough a confrontation arose among the men. Rising voices, faces flushing bright red, and finger jabbing had commenced—the prerequisites for a good old-fashioned brawl.

"On second thought, let's not." Eunice and I did a 180 degree turn and returned to our original position. I didn't want to get accidentally punched and obviously neither did Eunice. In such cases, retreat is the only answer.

The men were shouting at each other, while their sweethearts tugged on their arms, begging them to quit making a scene. The band stopped playing, and everyone gathered in the foyer to watch the oncoming melee. Some of the younger folks pulled out their phones to record. Again—let's record a fight rather than stop it. This is why I have such a dim view of humanity.

Don't get on your high horse and belittle me for not defusing the situation either. I have slain enough dragons in the past five years to last a lifetime. I've got a bad leg, a hearing aid, and failing kidneys to prove it. Franklin, Matt, and Baby have been shot because of me.

To say I am skittish around angry men is putting it mildly.

11

A sharp bugle's call pierced the din begging *attention*.
We stood transfixed in place and every eye sought the bugler. He was parked at the top of the grand staircase where Lady Elsmere stood flanked by Charles dressed as General Ulysses S. Grant and Rod, dressed as General Robert E. Lee, complete with beards and all. June looked resplendent in her dress and pearl tiara.

Everyone clapped as they gathered at the foot of the staircase to watch the trio descend. At the midway landing, they stopped and Charles gave a very short speech about unity and healing the nation's wounds. After he finished, June thanked everyone for participating, visiting, and volunteering for the reenactment. She raised her fist and her final words were "Let's party!" She motioned for the band to play again.

I glanced over at the buffet. The group of men had dispersed. Curry and Skeeter were nowhere to be seen. I searched for Rod who was making his way toward the elevator and went over to him. "Rod, how do you feel?"

Ignoring my question, he said, "Josiah. You are as pretty as a picture."

"I wish I could say the same about you. You don't look so good."

"I'm feeling a bit puny. Can you assist me back to my room? I need to get out of this heavy uniform and get back into my usual one."

"Rod, if you're not feeling well, lie down. I can bring you a plate of food."

Rod sucked his lower lip between his teeth. I could tell he was in pain.

"I'd like to, but Lady Elsmere was kind enough to let me stay here until Monday. I want to repay her kindness. I feel I should attend the ball."

"Listen to me. The Statler brothers are here and up to no good. You're not feeling well. You wobbled coming down the stairs. Do yourself a worthy turn and rest."

Rod's jaw clenched. "Those no-count boys are here?"

"Please don't spoil Lady Elsmere's party with your feud. Her Ladyship doesn't have too many more parties left in her. I want this to be a fond memory for her. She has worked very hard on this event and spent a great deal of money on it."

Rod's expression dulled in defeat. "All right. I'll go to my room and rest. I am tired and would appreciate something other than Civil War rations. I've had nothing to eat but hardtack, cornbread, and potatoes for the past several days. A tasty meal sounds good. Maybe that will perk me up."

"You go on. I'll bring you a nice plate of hot food."

Rod patted my shoulder. "Okay, Josiah. Have it your way." He turned and went into the elevator.

I pressed the second floor button for him and closed the gate. "Send the elevator back down when you get out."

Rod didn't answer. He seemed distracted.

I went in search of Charles and found him puffing on cigars with the mayor and several Lexington council members on the back patio. "General Grant, may I speak with you?"

"Excuse me, gentlemen. A lady beckons." We stepped out of hearing range of the city officials.

"Did you know that the Statler brothers are here?"

"Yes, I've got security keeping an eye on them, and we've notified the police that they are here. That's all we can do at the moment. I don't want to cause a scene."

"They sure have some moxie."

Charles nodded. "Like I said, I'm not going to do anything unless they create a situation. They are currently wandering about the corn maze, probably stealing candy from the children."

I chuckled.

"Where's Mr. Hiller?"

"He's taking a lie-down. I don't think he feels well. I'm about to take a plate to him."

Charles' eyebrows knitted together. "That's good. I appreciate you helping with him. We've rented a car, and he should be leaving Monday."

"I don't know if that's a good idea. I think Rod should go back to the doctor. He's looking mighty peaked. I thought he was going to stumble coming down the staircase."

"I'll talk to Mr. Hiller in the morning and take it from there. It's no hardship if he stays a few more days. Don't worry about him, Jo. We'll take care of the situation."

"Where's Her Ladyship?"

"Holding court in the ballroom and having the time of her life. Amelia and Bess are with her."

Satisfied that things were under control, I curtsied. "Thank you for speaking with me, General Grant."

"My pleasure, milady." Charles bowed and went back to the mayor, who was happily getting sloshed from drinking too many Mint Juleps.

I hurried to the buffet table where I waited in line for my turn. I fixed two plates and hijacked a server, who carried a tray with the plates heaping with food including desserts and drinks. I thought I would eat with Rod, giving him some company. It was a tight squeeze for the two of us in the elevator but we ascended to the second floor even though the machine complained, sounding like metal being stripped. That lift really needed to be replaced.

Knocking on Rod's door, I said, "Rod, it's me. Josiah. I'd like a private word with you."

No answer.

I knocked again. "Rod. I've brought a tray of food for us."

No answer.

I gingerly opened the door and poked my head in the bedroom. "Rod?"

No response. No one was in the room.

The server entered the room and laid down the tray. I dismissed him after thanking him, knowing that the server would be sorely missed downstairs.

Concerned, I checked the bathroom. Again, no sign of Rod. I felt the sink. It was dry, so he hadn't used it recently. In the wastebasket were tissues covered with a dark substance. I picked one tissue up and tentatively sniffed it. It had an odor similar to my face makeup. The false beard was also thrown into the wastebasket. I assumed the dark substance had something to do with the beard. Hmm?

I moved to the closet where I spied the Confederate uniform, so Rod must have changed. I hastily checked all the other bedrooms, but they were all locked, as was the custom when June had parties.

Where could Rod be?

I took the elevator back downstairs and peeked into

the ballroom. Lots of couples were dancing. I spotted Shaneika and Mike taking a chance on a quadrille. Shaneika gave me a quick wave before concentrating on the intricate steps of the dance. I saw Mike turn in the wrong direction. He was as confused as Shaneika, but they both seemed to be having fun. I made a quick sweep around the ballroom, but didn't see Rod. Perhaps he wanted some air before he turned in, or maybe Rod went looking for the Statler brothers.

I stopped by Lady Elsmere's dais where she was enthroned in a red velvet chair. "Having fun?" I said, raising my voice over the music.

"Having a ball," she answered, mischievously.

"Yuck, yuck."

"Come sit by me."

"I can't. I'm looking for Rod. Have you seen him?"

"Not since he escorted me down the staircase. Is something wrong?"

"Not really. Just wanted to check on him."

Amelia, who was sitting next to June, tapped her shoulder and pointed with a lace fan toward the foyer.

June looked around me, frowning. "Who's that, for goodness sake?"

I turned and saw a Grim Reaper with a real scythe standing in the entrance of the ballroom. The costume surprised me as the invitations stated Civil War attire only.

Amelia stepped off the dais. "I'll check it out. I

think I should inform Daddy."

June insisted, "Who was it?"

"I don't know. Whoever it is has on a mask," I replied. "I think I should go with Amelia." I needn't bothered to have answered as June was already engrossed in a lively conversation with one of her oldest friends. Oh well! I followed closely on Amelia's heels, but the Grim Reaper had disappeared.

"I'm going to alert security and Daddy. I didn't like the fact *our friend* was wearing a mask."

"You're worried about the mask and not the scythe?"

"Good point. If you see the guy, let security know."

"Sure thing," I answered distractedly. My attention was elsewhere as I spied Baby through the glass doors romping with the children. Oh, no!

Now how did that dog get out of the Butterfly? I certainly wanted to get my dog back home before he lunged on the buffet table in search of a treat or grabbed hold of some woman's skirt with his teeth, wanting to play tug of war.

I hurried outside and lifted a little girl off Baby's back. She was dressed like Shirley Temple in *The Littlest Rebel,* ringlets and all.

"Young lady, you're too big to be riding this dog."

Pursing her lips, the little girl stomped her foot. "He's not a dog. He's my pony, and I want to ride him."

"Baby is a dog—an English Mastiff, and you will hurt his spine if you ride him."

"No, I won't!"

"You're not riding this dog. Get lost, kid."

The little girl burst into tears and went screaming for her mother.

I told you I was good with kids.

Now for the dog.

"Baby, come here. We have to go home."

Baby took one look at me and loped into the corn maze. Apparently, Baby wasn't finished having fun.

"Baby, come here. I mean it."

My dog blissfully kept going.

I muttered, "I hate you sometimes, Baby." Resigned, I took a deep breath, picked up my skirts, and marched into the maze in search of my uncooperative canine. The maze was lit by solar lights placed in straw bales along the way, but the light still cast creepy-looking shadows on the corn rows. However, I was cheered by the candy stations I found along the way. The sugared nuts weren't bad.

"Baby! Baby! Treats! Treats!" I knew he would like the nuts. Baby had a sweet tooth.

As I was rounding a corner, Lincoln ran into me almost knocking me down. His eyes were wide with fright, and he pulled on my arms. "Come! Come away!"

I grabbed him tightly by the shoulders. "What is it, Linc?"

Looking beyond me, Lincoln shuddered and wrestled away from me, leaving me in the dust as he ran away. I turned to see what was troubling Lincoln when I spied the upper part of a scythe moving across the tops of the corn sheaths. It gave me a start.

If June had hired actors to frighten guests in the corn maze, she didn't bother to notify Amelia or any of her staff. I was very puzzled. I knew the Grim Reaper would soon encroach upon my row, so I tiptoed to another part of the maze, listening for other people and my dog. I wasn't quite sure if I should be wary. If June had hired someone to scare the bejeebies out of her guests, she didn't remember it when the Grim Reaper showed up in her ballroom. She seemed genuinely surprised, but June was known for playing games. This was a game, wasn't it?

With all the mayhem that had happened over the past several days, my nerves were frayed, so I decided to skip the rest of the ball entirely and go home, but I had to find Baby first. I glanced at the full moon before moving down the intersecting pathways. Where was that dog?

Baby howled. Somewhere deep in the maze, Baby howled again, and he didn't stop howling.

My heart froze.

I know my dog, and that was a howl was of desperation and fear. He needed help. I cried out, "BABY, MOMMY'S HERE!" I ran, or rather shuffled, down one path and then another following the sound of his cries until I chanced upon him. Baby was standing over something which I couldn't make out. Since Baby was agitated and can't see very well with only one eye, I held out my hand so he could sniff me. "It's me, Baby. It's me."

Recognizing my scent, Baby wagged his tail.

"Good boy. Good boy." Grabbing hold of his collar, I pulled Baby off whatever he was standing over. I bent closer, peering at what seemed to be a scarecrow dressed in a Confederate uniform. A cloud drifted over the moon, making it more difficult for me to see. I took a solar light from a straw bale and studied the form more closely.

Was it a dummy? I gingerly poked the form with my shoe which came away with blood on it.

Oh, my goodness! It was a person! This was no scarecrow!

It's hard for me to kneel, so I had to lean on Baby to get close enough to feel for a pulse. That is until Baby growled. Jerking my head up, I spotted the Grim Reaper standing motionless at the end of the path, quietly observing me.

"I need help. This person is injured."

The reaper swung the scythe around as though he was to cut a row of wheat or someone's head off, marching toward me. The only thing that sprang to mind was "Danger, Will Robinson. Danger!" from the

Lost In Space TV show. I don't know how I sprung up, but the next thing I remember I was running with Baby nudging from behind trying to get around me. It was every woman or dog for her/himself.

I quickly glanced over my shoulder only to see the Reaper giving chase. I ran across the lawn, through a crowd smoking on the patio, and burst into the ballroom, screaming, "Death! Death in the corn maze!"

Do I know how to party or what!

12

That was why I got arrested for murder. Or was it accessory to murder? I can't remember.

The police have never liked me, especially Detective Drake. I do see why they are suspicious since I have a penchant for stumbling over corpses. They really took offense when the local paper hailed me as the Bluegrass' very own Miss Marple. Might as well have put a bull's-eye on my back. The police are quite jealous of who takes credit for solving murders. They don't like amateurs stealing their thunder.

The police were called after the man was confirmed dead by Charles. They came, cordoned off the corn maze, took pictures, interviewed guests, searched the grounds, and arrested me.

My heart attack ruse didn't work. Kelly threw me in the back of a squad car and brought me to police headquarters, where he deposited me in an interview room—one that I had been interrogated in many times before.

"Don't you dare cuff me to that nasty desk," I said to Kelly, flecks of spit flying from my mouth.

Kelly looked pained. "This is standard procedure now."

"I'm wearing a long skirt with crinolines. I have no money. You've taken my shoes. I limp when I walk. How am I supposed to escape?"

He hesitated. "Okay, but I'm going to get into trouble for this."

"I don't care. I'm a victim. Not a murderer. This is a revenge tactic from Drake. He doesn't like it that I get more publicity than he does for solving murders."

"You don't care if I get into trouble?"

"No, not at the moment. As soon as I have the chance I'm going to call your mother and tell her about your disgraceful conduct toward me."

That put the lid on the kettle. Kelly stomped out of the room. A few seconds later I heard angry voices in the hallway. It was Drake and Kelly going at it. The arguing stopped and a door slammed.

In walked Drake looking all bothered. His blue polka dot tie was loosened, and it barely covered a ketchup stain on his crumpled white shirt. What male over the age of twelve wears a polka dot tie, I ask you?

"Mrs. Reynolds. Another body, eh. They do keep piling up around you."

"It's a gift." I could barely look at Drake, I hated the man so much. He had given me nothing but grief since he had taken over for my friend, Detective Goetz, in the department. He was constantly pulling me downtown for "interviews." It was not my fault I kept stumbling over corpses. It was a knack.

"A gift? More like a curse. You're the Typhoid Mary of murders, you know."

I didn't reply.

"Do you know why you are here?"

"Would it be because you are a petty bureaucrat?"

That really got under Drake's skin. His mouth set in a hard line, making his lips all the thinner. "You were the last person to see Skeeter Statler alive. You have blood on your shoes."

"I'm not talking to you, Drake. I'm waiting for my lawyer."

"You're pleading the fifth?"

"I'm waiting for my lawyer. That's all. So take your little folder filled with horrible photos of the dead man and hastily written notes filled with incorrect information and vamoose. I have nothing to say to you."

"You'll have to speak with me sooner or later. I'm the primary on this case."

"It will be later then."

"You act as though you don't like me, Josiah."

"Don't call me by my first name. We are not colleagues. We are not friends. Show some respect."

"Like you show me?"

I leaned forward and put my elbows on the table,

resting my chin on the top of my clasped hands. "This is personal for you. I mean, I get under your skin. Do you have a crush on me, Detective Drake?"

Drake made a sour face. He grabbed his folder and was moving to leave when Shaneika burst through the door.

"Detective Drake, I thought we had an understanding that Mrs. Reynolds was never to be interrogated without her lawyer present."

"I wasn't interrogating Mrs. Reynolds. We were having a friendly chat."

"Josiah, what have you told him?"

"Nothing. I was waiting for you, but I've been arrested."

Shaneika's eyes bore holes into Drake. "On what charge?"

"There has been a misunderstanding. Mrs. Reynolds was brought here to get her witness statement."

Shaneika took a recording device from her briefcase and placed it on the table. "Please identify yourself and restate the police's intention toward Josiah Louise Reynolds regarding the murder of Skeeter Statler."

"I'm Detective Drake. Mrs. Reynolds was brought to police headquarters to get her witness statement."

"Was Mrs. Reynolds handcuffed?"

"I believe she resisted."

"How many attendees from the Remembrance Ball were either handcuffed or asked to come to police headquarters to answer questions?"

Drake didn't answer.

"None, Detective Drake. Just my client. I think I've made my point."

"Mrs. Reynolds has blood on her shoes. She was the last person to emerge from the corn maze."

"Mrs. Reynolds leaned over the victim to help, which makes her a witness, not a suspect."

"Yeah. What she said." I sneered, having to get in my two cents worth.

Drake pushed on. "I would like to ask questions that might help with the investigation."

"As long as it is understood that my client is ready to help the police any way she can and is no way a suspect in the murder of Skeeter Statler."

"As of this moment, Mrs. Reynolds is a witness."

"Mrs. Reynolds, do you feel up to answering Detective Drake's questions?"

I was leaning sideways in my chair from fatigue.

Shaneika elbowed me to sit up straight and said to Drake, "Keep it brief."

"Can you tell me the events leading up to discovering Mr. Statler from tonight's ball?"

"Last night's ball," I said.

Drake looked at his watch. "Yes, last night's ball."

"I arrived at the Big House a little after seven. Franklin Wickliffe was with me. We talked with Lady Elsmere and then joined guests, who were arriving."

"Where was Lady Elsmere?"

"Still in her bedroom. Her Ladyship didn't join the party until eight-forty-five, more or less. I wasn't wearing a watch, so I have to guess the time."

"Then what happened?"

"Lady Elsmere made her appearance."

Drake looked at his notes. "Something happened before then. The Statler brothers arrived and caused a commotion. Weren't they invited?"

"All reenactors were, but the Statler boys caused a stir because they were wearing uniforms not permitted."

"Wasn't this a costume party?"

"Yes, but apparently there is a hierarchy. You have to go through the ranks like a real soldier if you're a reenactor."

"Didn't Rodney Hiller escort Lady Elsmere wearing a general's uniform?"

"Listen, you're gonna have to ask a reenactor these types of questions. I don't know all the rules pertaining to uniform apparel."

"I see that Mr. Hiller had an altercation with the Statler brothers yesterday and previously at the farmers' market."

"Yes, I witnessed it."

"Did Mr. Hiller make threats against them?"

"He said something like if they touched him again, he'd throw them in the gutter. Something like that.

Why don't you ask about how they threatened him? One of his buddies took a video of it."

"Did you see Mr. Hiller with the Statler brothers at the ball?"

"No. In fact, Rod retired to his room when he realized the Statler brothers were attending."

Drake studied his notes. "Where was Mr. Hiller's room?"

"On the second floor, down the hall from Lady Elsmere's room."

"Was anyone else staying as a guest?"

"I don't know. You'd have to ask her."

"What happened after Lady Elsmere came down the staircase?"

"Everyone had a great time. Then the Grim Reaper showed up."

"How was the Grim Reaper dressed?"

"You know, like a grim reaper—long brown robe, hood, mask, and a real scythe. He was creepy."

"Again, this was a costume party near Halloween."

"The invitations specifically said that everyone was to dress as a Civil War character. I don't know how many times I have to say it."

Shaneika reached into her purse and pulled out her invitation. "Here you go, Detective Drake. You may keep that."

"Perhaps Lady Elsmere hired this person to add a little oomph to the party?"

"You'd have to ask her. My catering company was hired for the food, decorations, flowers, and children's activities. Mr. DuPuy took care of security. Neither Mr. DuPuy nor Lady Elsmere ever said anything about hiring outside actors. I was very surprised to see this character. That scythe wasn't fake. It was real. He was creepy."

"You already said he was creepy. I get it. The Reaper was creepy."

"Well, he was."

"What made you go into the corn maze?"

"My dog, Baby, ran into the maze. I went after him."

"Was he invited as well?"

I made a face. "Noooo. Baby got out of my house, so I went in the maze to retrieve him and take him home."

"Let's start with when you went into the maze."

"I ran into Lincoln Todd. He seemed frightened and begged me to run with him. In fact, he tugged on me trying to get me to leave with him."

The detective glowered at Shaneika. "You know anything about this?"

"I haven't had a chance to talk with my son yet. He is with my mother. You may interview him after I speak with him. Of course, I'll be present for that interview too." She slid her business card toward Detective Drake. "Make an appointment. Don't show up unannounced at my door."

"Can we get back to the Grim Reaper?" I protested.

"You have my full attention, Mrs. Reynolds. I await your statement with bated breath."

"Okay. I went into the maze, ran into Lincoln, he ran off, and then I heard Baby howl. Now this wasn't just any howl. It was a terrified howl."

"How would you know that?"

"I know my dog's language, just the way a mother knows what her little baby is communicating to her."

"Go on. Your dog was terrified."

"He was telling the world that something was not right. I found him standing over something. At first, I thought it was a prop scarecrow that had fallen."

"You said Baby was standing over the body. Perhaps Baby knocked the man down?"

"Mastiffs stand over something or a person to guard—just like they sleep in doorways. It's instinctive to them. Did you know that Mastiffs were brought to Rome by Julius Caesar to fight in the arena? They guarded the entrances to castles in the medieval ages."

Shaneika nudged me.

Oh dear, I seemed to be rattling off target. I felt discombobulated like I was in a canoe on a fast running river with no oars. It's always alarming to discover a corpse. Readjusting my narrative, I continued, "I pulled Baby away from the scarecrow and then poked it with my shoe. That's how I got the man's blood on me and realized it was a person—not a prop."

"Did you check for a pulse?"

"Yes. The body was still warm."

Drake made a note. "Witnesses said you ran out of the corn maze screaming and I quote, 'Death! Death in the corn maze.'"

"Did I? I don't remember."

"Why did you assume murder?"

"Because a scythe-swinging maniac was chasing me."

"The corn maze was searched and no one in a Grim Reaper outfit was discovered. We have only your word that someone else was in the maze."

"But you did find a body?"

"Yes. It was Skeeter Statler and he is quite dead."

"How did he die?"

"We're not giving out that information at the moment."

"Which means that I'll read about in the paper today," I commented, referring to the constant leaks in the police department.

Drake frowned. "I can do without the insults."

"You dragged me down here in handcuffs and talk about insults." I turned to Shaneika. "Can we sue the police about this?"

"I can certainly look into it."

Drake threw up his hands. "Listen, I'm just trying to get to the bottom of this murder. Let's catch a killer first before you sue anyone."

"What else do you need to know?"

"You said the Grim Reaper chased you."

"He did. He first came at us swinging that scythe."

"Up and down?"

"No, sideways. Like cutting wheat or hay. Slicing motions. And he kept swinging when chasing Baby and me."

"How do you know that? You said you were running."

"I looked back and saw him."

"To whereabouts in the maze?"

"He chased me to the entrance. I could hear him behind me."

"You refer to it as he. Why?"

"He was tall like a man and bulky. I don't think it was a woman. I'm sure it was a man."

"I find it hard to believe that anyone can run and swing a scythe at the same time."

"He wasn't running when he first approached us. He walked toward us menacingly swinging."

"You're backpedaling."

"I'm exhausted. I need to rest and check on Baby. Are you going to arrest me?"

"Like you said—you're a witness. That is unless we find evidence to the contrary."

"I'm done." I stood and walked out the door.

Shaneika followed and took me home.

Baby greeted me at the front door with his tail wagging.

I took a pair of shears and cut off the nineteenth-century gown with gleeful abandon, as I couldn't unhook myself. Free from that prison of a dress, I took a shower and went nighty-night.

Traumatized and shivering, Baby jumped into bed with me.

I spooned Baby with my arms around my furry friend until I heard his rhythmic breathing. Knowing that Baby had fallen asleep relaxed me, but I still kept feverishly mulling over the day's events.

Come on, Mr. Sandman. Sprinkle a little sand on my eyes. I need to sleep, too.

13

I awoke after the sun was high in the sky. Oh, no! I was late for the morning cleanup. After checking on my animals, I hurried to the Big House. Eunice and Sharlene were busy cleaning.

"I thought everything would have been done by now," I said, looking about the mess.

Eunice said, "The police wouldn't let us in the house until noon." She handed me a trash bag. "Here you go."

"Any sign of the occupants?"

"Lady Elsmere is in her room having the vapors. Amelia and Bess are taking the day off."

"Has anyone fed June?"

Sharlene said, "I took a tray up to her first thing. I think she's quite upset about the ball."

"I'll check on her later," I said, throwing discarded napkins and dried out fruit into my trash bag.

Sharlene took a tray filled with dirty champagne flutes into the kitchen.

I sidled up to Eunice and whispered, "Have you seen Rod Hiller?"

"No, but the police came here this morning looking for him."

"They wanted to talk with him?"

"Badly. They took more pictures, interviewed Sharlene and me, and left several hours ago. They said we could finish cleaning."

"Who was here?"

"Detective Kelly and several uniform cops."

"Did they go into the corn maze?"

"Look, Josiah, we've got to get the house shipshape before four this afternoon. It's in our contract. We can talk about the murder later."

"You're right. Let's get to it. Tell me what you need for me to do."

"What you're doing. Pick up the trash."

That's what I did. Anything that could be stored in the fridge was done last night, so Eunice concentrated on breaking down the buffet table. Sharlene washed and put away the dishes, and I went from room to room, picking up trash with a trusty picker-upper thingy. I found two expensive earrings from mixed sets, a cameo brooch, quite a few buttons, one pair of sunglasses, one credit card, used napkins, used handkerchiefs, six kepi hats, three sets of women's white satin gloves, one set of men's tan leather gloves, one feathered hat, one tube of lipstick, and a discarded pair of pantaloons. I'm not even going to go there about the pantaloons.

I put the items on a table near the front door as I knew people would be stopping by to retrieve their belongings, especially the jewelry and the credit card. And they did. All afternoon, guests stopped by to reclaim their belongings and chit-chat with June, who was receiving in her bedroom. June's constant request for tea and cakes for her guests was wearing thin. I finally had to put a stop to guests visiting June as I couldn't get my work done.

Retrieving a vacuum from the hall closet, I commenced to sweeping June's expensive Persian rugs while Sharlene cleaned the ballroom with a four-foot long janitor's broom/mop and Eunice stacked chairs.

We finished just as Bess and Amelia came through the back kitchen entrance. Amelia went to June's room immediately as Bess inspected the downstairs, going through each room carefully. Bess was responsible for the inside of the Big House while her father took care of the outside. She knew June was very particular of how the Big House looked—wanting a tidy and orderly abode. After all, the Big House had a reputation of cleanliness, hospitality, and Southern charm to uphold, even if the dead bodies piled up.

Satisfied with our work, Bess wrote us a nice big check and bid us goodbye. She had dinner to prepare for Her Ladyship and family. I gave the check to

Eunice to deposit at the bank on Monday. After thanking Sharlene for her help, I took the elevator to the second floor and poked my head in June's room.

"You up?"

"Come in, darling girl." June wore a red velvet dressing gown and bright red lipstick. With her alabaster skin and white hair, she looked like a peppermint.

I sat on June's bed. "You're chipper today."

"Having myself an awfully good time."

"You do know a man died in your corn maze."

June shrugged, saying, "Dreadful. Simply dreadful."

"Aren't you worried about your reputation?"

"I'm eighty-eight. What do I care about my reputation?"

"I think Lincoln witnessed something important. He's distressed."

"That's most unfortunate. This will be his second murder. Not good for a person of such a tender age." Lincoln had previously witnessed the murder of Arthur Aaron Green, a former lover of June's.

I reached over and held June's hand. "I need for you to be serious. This is not one of your games. What was between Rod Hiller and Jimmy Ray Statler?"

June sighed and pulled her hand away. "Why won't the past stay buried?"

I waited for June to collect her thoughts.

"So many people in my life throughout the years—and so much wickedness. I'm not talking the usual weakness of human nature, but premeditated evil. There's evil everywhere, Josiah. Even in the nicest of people."

I shuddered. June seemed awfully serious. "What do you know, June?"

"Some things I know. Others I am surmising. It's not going to stop. Evil never does."

"Some? Others? What are you talking about? Tell me, June."

June mused about the past, mentally waving cobwebs from her mind. So many people. So many years ago. "I should never have fired Jimmy Ray."

"Why did you?"

"Rod was the farm manager then. I was just getting the farm on its feet, and he was a great help. I trusted him." June broke off.

"And?"

"He came to me with a story that Jimmy Ray Statler was stealing truck and tractor parts and selling them on the black market. I checked the inventory against invoices. Rod was correct. We were missing parts."

"Why did he think it was Jimmy Ray stealing?"

"He said it was only on Jimmy Ray's shift that the parts would go missing. Of course, I believed Rod and had him fire Jimmy Ray."

"Let me guess. The pilfering continued."

"It did, until I installed a computer tracking system in the repair shop."

"Rod quit."

"Yes. Completely. It wasn't until a year later I understood the situation, and that I had been so stupidly hoodwinked. When I read in the paper Rod had married Honoria, Jimmy Ray Statler's former wife, the pieces of the puzzle fell into place."

I was gobsmacked.

"Josiah, I know it is hard to accept since you like Rod so much, but he's a scoundrel. He was having an affair with Honoria, but she wouldn't divorce Jimmy Ray. To make Jimmy Ray small in Honoria's eyes, Rod framed him, hoping I would fire him."

I stated, "But Rod liked the money made from the stolen parts and kept it up."

"I think that's what happened."

"Did you confront him?"

"I had gone to see my lawyer about it when Rod got word and quit. Since I was new to the community, I didn't want a scandal, so I let it go. Now I wish I hadn't. Maybe if I had gotten the law involved, the tragedy in the corn maze wouldn't have happened." June forced a smile. "There is evil in the nicest of people—even me."

"Your actions were not evil, June. We all make decisions based on facts at a given time. You did nothing improper."

June winced as she wrung her hands. "I don't know, Jo. I really don't know. I should have rehired Jimmy

Ray, but he had started drinking and moved to Lincoln County. His life was in ruins—his marriage was busted and Honoria refused to take the two boys. Jimmy Ray had custody, but he was in no shape to take care of those youngins."

"Honoria didn't want her children?"

"She and Rod were besotted with each other. There was no room for anyone else."

I had to agree. They were a devoted couple who did everything together. "How do you know Honoria didn't want custody of her children?"

"Through mutual acquaintances. It was common knowledge."

"If you knew this, why did you underwrite the Civil War reenactment? You must have known Rod was a reenactor."

"My sponsoring the reenactment had nothing to do with Rod, but when I learned he was going to participate, I tried to establish boundaries with him."

"Like having him escort you down the staircase at the ball? I'm not getting this."

"I never knew the Statler boys had been giving Rod problems until the brawl at the farmers' market. By then it was too late. I had already committed to the reenactment and money had been spent. The program was very important to Charles, who wanted to use it as a teaching instrument to educate the public. He thinks lack of knowledge is the cause of so much unrest today."

"You did this as a favor for Charles?"

"Yes, but he knew nothing about Rod or the Statlers. Charles came to work for me the year Rod left." June paused for a moment. "I wanted to get a handle on this situation, so that's why I invited Rod to stay and escort me down the staircase. It was to keep him on a leash. Security was to keep an eye on him and the Statler brothers."

"Your security failed miserably."

"I'll say," June concurred. "That's why I wanted to talk with guests stopping by this afternoon. It was to glean information from them. You know how people love to gossip."

I inwardly cringed at the number of guests I stopped from visiting June. How was I to know she was secretly interrogating them. "Now what?"

"I'm working in the dark. I don't know which brother was killed or if it was really murder."

"It was Skeeter Statler."

June asked, "What about Curry?"

"I don't know. The police are looking for him. Have they talked with you?"

"Not yet."

"Do you think Rod was involved?"

June looked weary. "I hope not."

"Did you talk with him after the ball?"

"Never saw him after he escorted me down the staircase."

"Who was dressed as the Grim Reaper?"

"I don't know. I never hired anyone to act as the Reaper. That costume was inappropriate to the party's theme. I was surprised as everyone else."

"Who's everyone else?"

"Well, Amelia and Bess for starters. Eunice said you didn't hire any actors for the corn maze, so I'm at a loss as to whom it could have been."

"You had security at the entrance. Any explanation of how he got in?"

"You'll have to ask them. Charles hired them."

"Is he around?"

"He's at the nursery barn today with the vet."

"I'll leave you to the tender mercies of Amelia and Bess. I need to skedaddle."

"Stop by tomorrow. I may have more information."

"I will. I promise."

I left June's room determined not to show her how disturbed I was. If she hadn't sponsored the Civil War reenactment, none of this mischief would have happened.

I was sure of it.

14

I found Charles in the mares' barn with the vet. They were testing to see if the mares were ready to breed. The vet was using an ultrasound machine to view the ovaries to pinpoint if a mare had released an egg during her heat cycle. If receptive to breeding, the mare would be checked for her overall health including venereal diseases.

In the Thorougbred business, money is made from breeding horses—not racing. Brood mares are bred every year, and if their reproductive system fails, they are sold off. That was something Lady Elsmere was trying to change. She bred her mares every other year, giving them a rest and pledged that all her brood mares retired on the farm. Unfortunately, many horse farms couldn't adopt Lady Elsmere's policies because they desperately needed the cash flow from yearling sales that brood mares provide.

I waited in the barn's office until Charles was free. He seemed surprised to see me. I'm sure he was worn down by my pestering him for information.

Charles said, "I see the police released you."

"Thanks for trying to protect me, but you shouldn't have threatened to punch a cop in the nose. The law takes a dim view of that."

"Cuffing you was ridiculous."

"What time did you get to bed?"

"Around five this morning."

"Isn't that when you usually get up?"

"It's been a rough several days, Josiah." Charles slumped in a chair and pulled a beer from a small refrigerator. "Want one?"

I shook my head. "You look tired."

"As soon as the vet leaves, I'm going to bed. I'm not a young chicken anymore."

"A nap sounds pretty good right now, but I've got bees to check myself. Before I leave, I would like to talk to your security for the party. What company did you hire?"

"We used our own people."

"What do you mean?"

"Our own guys from the farm. I hired an outside firm for the reenactment, but for the party, we used staff. They work parties for overtime, and we are glad to give them the work."

"I see. Is there a particular person in charge?"

"Yes. Talk to Manuel at the repair shop."

"Okay, I will. One more thing, Charles."

"Yeah?"

"Please don't sponsor another Civil War reenactment. I can't handle the stress."

Charles grinned and took a long drink from his beer can.

I took my leave and went to the repair shop, asking for Manuel. A smallish, middle-aged man with black hair, wearing a black sleeveless shirt that showed off a Semper Fi tattoo on his upper arm. He wiped grease from his hands with an old rag.

"Hi. Are you Manuel?"

"Yes ma'am."

"I am Josiah Reynolds. I own the farm next door."

"I know who you are. I've seen you with Her Ladyship. You own that big dog."

"Yes, his name is Baby."

"He comes over sometimes."

"I hope he's not a bother."

"He likes to be petted. I keep treats for him. Baby is partial to beef jerky." Manuel put his shop rag in his back pocket. "I like dogs."

"That's very kind of you."

"Now those peacocks of yours are a different matter. They come over and poop on our vehicles. We like to keep our equipment clean." Manuel glared at me.

Yikes! Not off to a good start. Changing the subject, I said, "I have some questions to ask you about the party last night. Mr. DuPuy said I might. May I?"

"If it's okay with the boss, it's okay with me."

"Mr. DuPuy says you were in charge of the party security."

"That's right."

"May I ask what makes you qualified?"

"I was a member of the Marine Raider Regiment. That's a special unit within the Marines, ma'am."

I knew of this unit. They were the elite of the elite. "How did you come to work for Lady Elsmere?"

"Got too old for the Marines and getting shot at didn't help either. I had a cousin who worked here, and he got me a job working on the machinery after I retired."

"It's a bit dull, isn't it—working here after being on tactical assignments all over the world?"

"Would you call last night dull, ma'am?"

"Touché. Can you tell me about the security protocol?"

"We had two men working the main gate where all invitees had to show their invitation. One man was assigned to reviewing the invitations and another man wrote down vehicle license plate numbers. The drivers were instructed to drive to the front door of the Big House, where they were met by valets, who parked the cars for them."

"What if the cars were driven by chauffeurs?"

"There were only four limousines with chauffeurs."

"Did the chauffeurs stay with the limousines?"

"Each chauffeur was given a basket of food with various non-liquor beverages provided by your catering company and instructed to stay with their vehicles. Each member of the security team was also given a basket provided by your catering company. It was very good chow. Everyone appreciated the gesture."

"What about calls of nature?"

"Mr. DuPuy rented porta-potties for us which were placed on the north side of the house out of sight of the guests."

"How many people were on the security team?"

"Fourteen."

"You've got two men on the gates. I take it the valets were part of your team."

Manuel nodded.

"What did the rest of the team do?"

"They patrolled the perimeter of the farm and made sure no one snuck off to the barns."

"What about the corn maze?"

"We had two people check the corn maze every twenty minutes. Several guests got lost in the maze and we helped them out."

"The men at the front gate. Did they report anyone showing up in a Grim Reaper outfit?"

"No."

"Are they sure?"

"I questioned them thoroughly as did the police. No one came to the ball dressed as a Grim Reaper."

"Did you see the Grim Reaper?"

"I didn't see him. We were not allowed in the Big House, but many guests and your staffers corroborated that a person in a Grim Reaper outfit did make an appearance at the ball."

"It would seem to me that between the front gate and the Big House's front door, someone changed into a Grim Reaper outfit. What's your theory?"

"Since the guests were let off at the front door, it is unlikely that any of them could have changed so quickly coming down the driveway. None of the valets say that a guest got out of a vehicle in the Grim Reaper outfit. Based on my information, I think these are the possibilities—one, a chauffeur changed into the outfit; two, the outfit was hidden in the trunk of a vehicle and a guest slipped out of the party to change; three, an unknown person entered the farm by unknown means."

"What about the staff? Did anyone have a beef with Lady Elsmere or the DuPuy family?" I was wondering if the farm staff had heard about June's checks to the DuPuys and a staff member was upset. June employed many people—horse trainers, vets, groomers, mechanics, handymen, office staff, tech people, fence menders, general farm workers, and more.

Manuel looked offended. "Everyone likes it here. We are blessed to be employed by Lady Elsmere. She just gave everyone on her staff a five thousand dollar bonus."

"When was this?"

"Last week."

It disturbed me that June was giving away all this money. Was she planning to die soon?

"No one saw the Reaper leave the corn maze? Can you explain that?"

"No, ma'am. The police think the Reaper changed out of the outfit, hid it, and blended in with the other guests."

"He still would have had to come out of the maze."

"No one would have noticed. All eyes were on you."

I blushed. "I guess I was screaming a little loudly."

Manuel deadpanned, "You were very *excited*, ma'am."

"Anything you would like to add?"

"No, ma'am, except that my crew is scouring the farm looking for that outfit."

I handed him my card. "If you find anything, please call me. I would appreciate it."

Manuel tucked the card in his front pocket. "I will if Mr. DuPuy says okay."

"Fair enough," I said, shaking Manuel's hand.

I left the repair barn more confused than ever. I had no idea of how the Grim Reaper got in and then escaped.

It had to be an inside job. Just had to be.

There was no other explanation for it.

15

After leaving the repair shop, I went to the corn maze. It was cordoned off, but you know me—I just ignored the yellow tape and went in. Right inside was a placard map of the maze. I studied it and then retraced my steps from the night before. It was tricky as now the sun was still shining and the maze was awash in sunlight. It was that last gasp of golden light before the gloaming. The maze had a totally different look to it as well as a dissimilar atmosphere. It wasn't as sinister, but I still wanted to get in and out before dark.

I carefully studied the ground and the inside walls of the maze until I came to the spot where I had found Skeeter Statler's body. I knew it was the correct spot as there was dried blood on the ground and broken corn stalks indicating there had been a scuffle. I wondered if Skeeter had defensive wounds on his hands. I pushed corn stalks apart hoping to find something—anything relating to this man's death. I checked both sides, finding nothing. The sun was setting over the horizon, causing the sky to darken. I needed to get home.

Leaves from mature pin oak trees, surrounding the Big House, were drifting downward on a soft breeze and littering the maze's pathways. I stooped to pick up several of the more colorful leaves, thinking it wouldn't be long before winter. I was on my way out when I spotted something snagged between a corn stalk and dried-up ear of corn. I peered closely before pulling it from the corn stalk. It was a piece of my yellow scarf I had given to Rod for a favor. Same color. Same material.

Reluctantly, I stuck the material in my coat pocket, knowing I would never share it with the police because they might use it to implicate me. Like I said before—I had slain my share of dragons. I was not going to let this dragon burn me to a crisp. I had discovered that the truth doesn't matter often times. Perception does.

I was the last person to run out of that corn maze. The police didn't find any evidence of a Grim Reaper inside the maze, but this little piece of material linked me to a man who held a grudge against the Statler brothers. Guilty by association.

Detective Drake would use that scarf to hammer me into the ground. Even if I could prove my inno-cence before charges were made, I still would have spent thousands of dollars on lawyers. It would be the financial ruin of me. Drake made no pretense of his dislike for me and would use the law to make me an example. What was so frustrating was that the law was on his side.

I didn't know what to do. Should I go on vacation and hope this would blow over by the time I got back? Should I continue investigating on my own and risk Drake's wrath if we crossed paths?

Was Skeeter Statler even murdered?

Was Curry Statler dead as well?

Did Rod Hiller dress as the Grim Reaper?

So many questions.

I needed answers.

And I needed them fast!

16

The next morning I read in the paper that Skeeter's death had been declared a death via blunt trauma to the skull. I reread the article carefully. No slice and dice? Someone hit Skeeter over the head. If the Grim Reaper didn't kill Skeeter with his scythe, then who did and with what?

Maybe I was going about this all wrong. I called Eunice's house.

"Hello."

"Eunice, this is Jo. Is Lincoln there?"

"He's at school."

"May I speak with him this afternoon?"

Eunice was emphatic. "No way. That boy has been through enough."

"I understand."

"I'm sorry. I didn't mean to sound so rude."

"You're his grandmother. You're supposed to protect him."

"I'm glad you understand. Shaneika and I want

things to go back to normal for him."

"Did the police interview Lincoln?"

"Early this morning before school."

"And?"

"Josiah, you're the worst."

"I know you were with Lincoln when he was interviewed."

"I watched."

"So tell me what he said."

"Not much. He and other kids were gathering candy in the maze. They heard a scuffle and some low-pitched moaning. The other kids ran away while Lincoln went in search of the moaning. He discovered the Grim Reaper leaning over the body of Mr. Statler."

"What happened then?"

"The Reaper heard Lincoln gasp and swung his scythe at him. Lincoln ran and bumped into you."

"I know the rest."

"I wish you'd give this a break. I'll talk to you later."

"Wait a minute. Wait a minute. Don't hang up."

"There's nothing more to tell."

"Did Linc see a rock or a large piece of wood near Statler's body?"

"No."

"Was he asked?"

There was a pause on the other end of the phone line. "Come to think of it, he wasn't."

"Did Lincoln see anyone else in the maze?"

"No."

"Was Baby with the body when Lincoln stumbled upon it?"

"I have no idea. He wasn't asked about Baby. Is it important?"

"I saw Baby run into the maze and went after him, and I didn't bump into any children running away. Just Lincoln."

"What are you implying?"

"I just find it odd that Lincoln didn't mention seeing Baby. The dog would have had to pass him in the maze."

"Not necessarily. Baby could have gone a different route than Lincoln or barreled through the corn."

I couldn't deny what Eunice said might be true. "I suppose."

"Don't talk about this murder around Lincoln. He's a very sensitive boy. I don't want this to warp him."

"Will you keep me informed if there are changed circumstances?"

"Such as?"

"Lincoln might remember something."

"I will but I'm not going to push his memory."

"I know I'm asking a lot."

"You sure are." Click.

I looked at my receiver. "Hello? Eunice?"

My business partner had hung up on me.

That was a first.

17

The next day I worked my bees in the back pasture. Behind the bee hives was a row of honeysuckle bushes and then the fence which separated my property from June's. All along the fence line, June and I had installed three electronic gates which opened via a sensor. This provided a convenient way to travel back and forth when using each other's pastures, which we were apt to do on special occasions.

I was worried by the weak hive I had noticed before the reenactment and needed to get inside. My guess was that the queen had become injured or died. I lit my smoker and took off the hive's outer and inner covers. Pulling out several frames, I discovered rows and rows of unborn bees. Sure enough, the queen was dead and a worker bee had taken her place laying unfertilized eggs which resulted in drones. In a hive, female worker bees are its lifeblood—male drones do not contribute to the stability of their own hive. They follow a virgin queen on her mating flight into the air where she will mate with many drones from all hives. If a drone is success-ful in mating with a queen, he dies. If the queen has successfully mated and is strong enough to reach her hive again, she will never leave it unless a new queen succeeds her or she dies. It's all about the collective—not the individual.

I selected my strongest hive and took off the outer and inner covers. Then I put newspaper on the top hive body and quickly replaced the inner and outer covers. I would come back after dark when the bees had settled and put the hive body of the weak bees on top of the newspaper of the strong hive. By the time the bees chewed through the newspaper, the weak hive would have accepted the queen of the strong hive. That's the goal, anyway.

After checking the hives, I looked at my watch. Time for lunch. As I was heading back, something glinted from under a honeysuckle bush. Curious, I went over to have a look-see only to recoil.

It was the scythe from the Grim Reaper!

How was I going to explain finding that scythe on my property to Detective Drake?

18

I slammed on my Prius brakes and skidded to a stop in Rod's gravel driveway. Knocking loudly on the front door and getting no answer, I went around back, calling his name.

Rod answered from his work shed, poking his head out from the door. A shadow crossed his face when he saw me, but I paid no never mind. I was loaded for bear.

"Josiah, what a pleasant surprise."

"Did you hear that I was handcuffed and carted downtown after Skeeter Statler was found dead?"

"Yeah, I did hear."

"And yet you never called to see how I was."

Rod looked sheepish. "I've been meaning to, but I've been so dad-burned busy."

"Don't hand me that crap."

"I don't know what you mean."

"I've caught on to you. I know all about your history with Jimmy Ray Statler."

Rod's eyes narrowed. "You better watch your mouth, missy."

"You better watch your back, Rod. I just might stick a knife in it."

"Not nice to threaten me, Josiah."

"I'm giving you warning that if you mess with me, you take on Asa as well. Remember my daughter, Asa? She eats punks like you for breakfast. And for that matter, so do I." I stepped closer to him with my hand on my stun gun hidden in my coat pocket.

Rod held up his hands in supplication. "Now hold on a minute. Let's start over. What's got a burr under your saddle?"

"I've worked it out, Rod."

"I don't know what you mean." Rod raised his eyebrows and protruded his bottom lip in an effort to look innocent. It was laughable.

"Two decades ago, you and Jimmy Ray Statler were hired by Lady Elsmere to help run her newly acquired farm. You thought she was an eccentric old lady with money to burn and decided to take advantage of her naivety. Both of you were in cahoots stealing machine parts and selling them on the black market—but here's the clincher. Lady Elsmere has always been very good with money, and she noticed too much being spent on replacing parts. So she started nosing around—asking questions. That's when you got the bright idea of turning the thefts around to your benefit. After all, you were sleeping with Jimmy Ray's wife, Honoria, and wanted to keep her."

"You keep Honoria out of this."

"You arranged for Jimmy Ray to take the blame alone. You framed him. Jimmy Ray loses his job and looks small in Honoria's eyes. A blood feud begins between the two of you and Honoria takes sides—she leaves Jimmy Ray for you. Just like you were hoping for."

"Josiah, you don't understand. It wasn't some cheap little affair. It was the love of a lifetime. Honoria and I were made for each other. We were truly happy, blissfully so, until she died. I don't regret a thing I did to win her."

"You didn't steal because of Honoria. You stole because you're a thief. You still kept stealing from Lady Elsmere, but quit when you thought she was going to expose you."

"It was as you say. I knew one afternoon that Lady Elsmere was going to fire me. I could tell from her demeanor that she suspected, so I beat her to the punch. I quit first."

"Tell me one thing—did Honoria know you let Jimmy Ray take the fall alone?"

Rod hung his head. "Not at first, but later."

I stepped back. "Wow, that's cold."

"Honoria wanted me as much as I wanted her. Jimmy Ray wouldn't let go, so I had to make him. It was that or kill him."

"But you killed Honoria's son, Skeeter."

"No. No. No. I had nothing to do with Skeeter's death. Nothing, you hear!"

"I came up to your room with a tray, but you weren't there. You had already changed out of your general's uniform and gotten into the Grim Reaper's outfit. You went into the corn maze where you had arranged a meeting with those boys and killed Skeeter on the spot. God only knows where Curry's body is. You better not have dumped him on my property like you did the Reaper's costume."

"Hold on, Josiah. You've got this all wrong. Let me walk you through the events of the past months. You'll see that I had nothing to do with that young man's death. I may be a thief and a scoundrel, but I'm not a murderer."

Rod guided me to chairs underneath a sycamore tree. Near the shade tree, there was a hatchet in a chopping block where he had been splitting wood. I pulled it out of the block and kept it with me for insurance. Now I had a stun gun and a hatchet. "Shaneika Mary Todd knows where I am, and if she doesn't hear from me every half hour, she is going to call the police."

"Give me a chance to explain."

"You've got ten minutes."

"Before she died, Honoria made me promise to get

in touch with her boys."

"For what purpose?"

"To see if they needed anything."

"Rather late in the day for that, wasn't it?"

"Jimmy Ray made it difficult for Honoria to see the boys. Turned them against her. But when he died, they had a change of heart. They contacted Honoria, but in the end, all they wanted was money. We didn't have any money to spare, so the boys stopped contacting her."

"Why did she want you to try again?"

"Guilt, I guess. We could have done more to stay in their lives, but we were too wrapped up in our own. Honoria felt bad about that."

"Honoria died three years ago."

"It took me time to get my bearings after she died. I finally contacted the brothers six months ago." Rod sighed.

"And?"

"They needed money and I needed money. Honoria's illness wiped me out. I had to mortgage the farm and was falling behind on the payments. This was a chance to get me out of the hole. It was a fast way to make a buck. Without Honoria to keep me on the straight and narrow I succumbed."

"To what?"

"After they made fools out of themselves by salting gold in streams, they had a proposal. It was Curry's idea. They wanted to create a storyline in which we pretended to feud. They would post online and get 'likes.' If they went viral, they might get their own show."

"I don't understand."

"It's like we were on a TV show. We were performing when we feuded over agate, fossils, fluorspar, just like on other reality shows. I told you mineral hunting is the new thing. That's why we needed the 'likes.'"

"You hired someone to film your encounters with the Statler brothers."

"Now, you're getting it."

"You get 'likes.' Then what?"

"The more 'likes' we get, the more popular we become until we go viral. Curry's plan worked like a charm. We were becoming stars. The sale of my agate was going through the roof, which allowed me to raise the prices. On top of that, their YouTube channel was raking in ad revenue. We even had a Hollywood agent call interested in doing a show with us. Two networks are looking for rock hounds to feature on a new reality rock hunting show. We were basically auditioning for it—creating a story."

"You're telling me that Curry and Skeeter never stole your agate."

"The fight at the farmers' market—it was all staged."

I said, "But the cuts and the bruises looked real."

"We had to make it look authentic."

"The shooting at the reenactment was staged."

"We thought it would make great footage, but something went wrong. Live ammunition was never to be used. I was not to be harmed. It was a prank, Josiah. Just a prank for the camera."

"Some prank, Rod."

"When I realized that Curry and Skeeter had used real ammo, I panicked. I was to meet them in the corn maze that night, but I chickened out. Went home with a reenactor buddy of mine who offered to let me stay at his house. That's where I've been for a couple of days. I didn't know Skeeter was dead until yesterday. I don't know what happened."

"What's your buddy's name? Was it Saginaw?"

"Yep, Saginaw Marshall. He'll verify that I was with him at the time of Skeeter's death."

"How do you know what time he died?"

"It had to be shortly after I escorted Lady Elsmere down the staircase. After I heard they were at the party, I went upstairs to change and then slipped out the side door. Saginaw and I went back to his place and ordered a pizza."

"What do you think happened?"

"I think the boys set up to murder me. They obviously blame me for taking away their mother and breaking up their family. They enticed me with my own greed."

I was quiet for a long time. Finally, I said, "I need to call Ms. Todd."

"What do you think, Josiah?"

"I think your story has large holes in it."

"I'm telling you the truth."

"Where is my yellow scarf, Rod?"

Rod looked around. "I don't know. Must have left it at the hospital."

I didn't mention Rod had gone to the corn maze and was wearing my scarf when he did so. He was lying to me. What other lies would he tell me? "Your story doesn't make sense. I haven't seen the ballistic reports, but the police think the gun that shot you is the one found in your own glove compartment. How did it get there?"

"Curry or Skeeter put it there."

"Then who was dressed up like the Grim Reaper? It makes more sense that you went upstairs, changed into the Reaper outfit, made an appearance in the Big House so everyone would see you and kept your appointment with the Statlers in the corn maze. There was an altercation. You picked up a rock and struck Skeeter."

"It makes more sense that Curry killed Skeeter. Where is he, Jo? Where's Curry?"

"I would say dead somewhere. Everything points to you, Rod. You've been to my house many times. You know about the electronic gates between June's property and mine. It would be nothing for you to sneak out of the corn maze and stash that outfit on my property and then run off to meet your buddy, Saginaw, and establish an alibi."

"I can't talk to you. You won't listen."

"I gave you a chance. You didn't tell me the truth."

Rod protested, "I did. Those boys double crossed me. It was supposed to be a game."

"Turned out to be a pretty deadly game."

Rod covered his face with his hands. "A giant mess is what I've gotten myself into."

I was outraged. "You used us. You used me. All because you wanted to sell more agate. Do you have any idea of how many lives you have impacted and not for the good? Greedy and selfish you are!"

He looked up. "Sorry. Sorry for it all. I didn't mean for things to get so carried away."

"You're sorry? Are you sorry about ruining Lady Elsmere's reenactment and the ball? She spent quite a bit of money on the project, not to mention you shamed her in public. What about all the reenactors and volunteers whose weekend was ruined? What about a young man dead in a corn maze? Or the traumatized child who saw the body?"

"None of that was supposed to happen. The altercation at the skirmish was to be playacting caught on film. It wasn't to interrupt the battle. In fact, we didn't think anyone would notice with all the chaos of a skirmish and cannons blasting away. Curry was to shoot the .22 with blanks, I was to fall as though I was hit, and then they were to blend back in with the Confederates."

"They both must have really hated your guts. They hated you for taking their mother away. They hated you for their miserable childhood. They played you, Rod, plain and simple." I stood, feeling bile rising up my throat. I wanted to vomit. I really did.

"Josiah, what are you going to do now?"

"I called the police about the costume. I'm sure they are in possession of it now. I would guess they will be coming to see you soon. Better get a good lawyer, Rod."

"This is a rough way to end a friendship. You were always good to me and Honoria. I'm sorry to see it end."

I didn't reply. Good riddance to a bad penny. You think you know someone, but one day you realize that you didn't know him at all.

19

Evil begets evil.

Isn't that what the good book says? There are dark powers and forces that work in this world, and we must be ever vigilant.

My problem was I didn't believe Rod. The story was too fantastic.

I pulled into my gravel driveway and pushed the codes to the gate. The police should be finished by now. I let Shaneika handle the search and seizure, as I wanted no contact with Detective Drake. But it was not to be.

There were two police cars with Detective Drake waiting with Shaneika in front of the Butterfly. Oh, great.

"We have a problem," Shaneika said.

"What is it?" I asked, wearily getting out of my car. I wanted nothing more than to eat a carton of ice cream, binge watch True Crime TV, and take a nap— the healing process of most women.

"We can't find the costume."

I glanced back and forth between Drake and Shaneika. Neither one was looking amused. "I told you exactly where it was."

Shaneika said, "It's not there."

"Making a false report is against the law," Drake said.

Searching my purse, I said, "Zip it, Drake."

Drake's brow furrowed.

I pulled out my phone and tapped on photos. I have to admit I love my new phone, but I still will not give up my landline. "There. See." I showed them a picture of the outfit in the bushes.

For once Drake didn't know what to say.

"I'll find out who stashed that costume and who stole it. I have a secret deer cam overlooking those hives. Have one of your men fetch it, and we'll take a looky-look."

It wasn't long before Drake and Shaneika stood behind me while I took out the memory card from the camera and inserted it into my computer. Various pictures of deer, possums, and raccoons dotted my screen. Then a human entered the screen, but it was too blurry to make an ID. All we could tell was it was a male. We watched several frames of the man shoving the scythe into the honeysuckle shrub and piling branches around it. Next were frames of more deer, a peacock, a nosy goat, and me working the hives. After me, crows pecked at the deer cam and then a man fumbling in the bushes for the scythe and costume. He looked right toward the camera.

"It looks like a different man took the Reaper outfit than the one who put it there," Shaneika commented.

"Any idea who the last guy is?" Drake asked.

Chagrined, I said, "His name is Manuel. He was in charge of the party security. He works for Lady Elsmere."

Drake flipped back several pages in his notebook. "We spoke with him on the night of the party."

"Looks like you're going to speak with him again. This I can tell you—the man who put the outfit on my property in the first place was not Rod Hiller. Rod is taller than the man in the frame." I ejected the memory card and handed it to Detective Drake. "I'm sure your people can clean the image up."

"Wanna take a guess?" Drake asked.

"I would say Curry Statler, but I can't make a positive ID. I would have guessed he was dead as well. Looks like I was wrong."

Drake said, "You're admitting that you were wrong. That's a first."

"Wonders never cease, Detective."

"What reason would Curry have for killing his brother?"

"I don't know. If I were you, I would have another talk with Rod Hiller."

"I intend to. Thanks for the card."

"I would like to know one thing. Was the gun in Rod's truck the one that shot him?"

"Yes."

"Who fired it? Curry or Skeeter?"

"Both of their prints are on the gun."

"But who shot it?"

Drake looked irritated. "You said one thing."

Shaneika ran interference for me. "Mrs. Reynolds just voluntarily gave you an important piece of evidence."

Drake shifted one leg and then another, deciding if he was going to comply. Finally, he said, "From the wound on Mr. Hiller's head, the shot must have come from Curry Statler. This is backed up from eyewitnesses."

"Thank you."

"One more thing, Mrs. Reynolds."

"Oh?" Please don't ask me where I was. Please don't ask me.

"Where have you been this afternoon?"

Darn. Darn. Darn. "I had things to do."

"Like?"

"Private things."

"Anything that pertains to this case?"

I winced. Lying to Drake about visiting Rod could get me in a lot of trouble.

"Mrs. Reynolds, where were you?"

"I went to see Rod Hiller."

Drake's face clouded up and expanded, making me think he was going to explode like a balloon. No, that's not right. He looked more like a puffer fish. Drake turned to Shaneika. "Just when I think Mrs. Reynolds is cooperating, she pulls a stunt like this."

"Is Mr. Hiller under suspicion for murder?" Shaneika asked.

"He's a person of interest."

Shaneika said, "Then you should talk with him. You've got your memory card. Let's take one thing at a time."

Drake stepped forward and pointed a finger in Shaneika's face. "You need to talk with your client about proper protocol. Reynolds is a busybody, and I'm going to lock her up if she doesn't stay out of my business."

"Point taken. Thank you for coming, Detective Drake. Let me escort you out." She locked his arm with hers and walked the seething detective to the front door with Baby padding after them.

I heard the front door slam.

A few minutes later, Shaneika strolled back in the office with Baby nudging her hand. "Detective Drake is very upset with you, Josiah."

"I gathered that."

"Drake's not the only one. I think he's right. You are too involved in this case and meddling with the investigation. It's gonna backfire. I could make a good case against you right now if I were a DA."

"For what?"

"An accessory."

"I showed proof that I didn't put the Reaper's outfit on my property."

"But you could have colluded with the murderer to hide it there."

"Why would I have called Drake about finding it if I'm guilty? Huh?"

"It wouldn't take much for a DA to turn the facts around and convince a jury otherwise."

"Shift the paradigm." I tapped my index finger on the desk. "We are missing a critical witness to all of this."

"Whom do you mean?"

"Remember that story where a serial killer was killing women in their homes during the day in a small community out west. No one saw a strange man in the neighborhood. The police couldn't believe that no one witnessed anything."

"What's your point?"

"The neighbors did see the killer. Even spoke to him, but didn't understand what they saw."

"Get on with it, Jo. I've got court soon."

"It was the mailman. Someone you see walking in your neighborhood every day, but take no notice of."

"What has that to do with this murder?"

"Who's the one person present at these events, but no one took any notice?"

Shaneika shrugged. "I don't know. Who?"

"The camera guy. I've been so focused on Rod that I forgot he and the Statler brothers hired a cameraman to film their encounters."

"It could have been a woman they hired or more than one person. Nowadays, anyone can film on their phone."

"I saw this guy at the farmers' market filming Rod and the Statler brothers' fisticuffs, and he was using a professional video camera. I saw him again at the Civil War reenactment. I bet he was at the ball secretly filming."

"Do you know this man's name?"

"No, but I can ID him. Who was taking lots of pictures that night?"

"Franklin did. So was Mom."

"I need to look at their pictures. I know I can identify this man. The police need to talk to him."

"I'll give them both a call right now, and then I need to scoot."

"I know. You have court."

"Gotta make money to pay the bills, Josiah—just like everyone else on God's green earth."

Don't I know it, honey. Don't I know it.

20

I thought I was home free. Shaneika Mary Todd discussed the existence of the camera man with Detective Drake and reported to me that they were looking for him as well as Curry, who was still at large. You know my thoughts on Curry. He was dead in a shallow grave somewhere. However, I felt I had done all I could have done to help the police. Now, I wanted my life back.

Shaneika was right. Finding the murderer of Skeeter Statler was the police's job—not mine. I needed to concentrate on happier issues. Murder was so dark and disturbing.

Hunter was due home in several days. June had bounced back from her funk and was planning her next party. The weak queenless bees settled nicely in their new hive. Asa, my daughter, called and said she was coming home for Thanksgiving. Things were looking up.

I went to the farmers' market as usual, set up my

booth at six in the morning, and plunked my big behind in a chair to take a break before the customers straggled in.

Our manager came to my booth collecting the booth fees. "Howdy, Jo."

"Good morning," I replied, handing him money. "Rod not coming today? He's usually set up by now."

"Doesn't look like it. Have you heard from him?"

"No, not since midweek."

"Heard he had a mishap at the reenactment."

"It was minor."

The manager looked irritated, which he usually was. Farmers are not the easiest group to get along with. It's rather like herding cats. We are tough, independent cusses who march to a different drummer. I know that's a cliché, but it's true.

"If he doesn't come in the next ten minutes, I'm going to put someone in his spot. Talk to you later," the manager muttered before he moved on.

Rod never showed.

We have a strict rule that all vendors must call the manager if they can't make the market. I didn't think anything about it since I believed Rod had taken off to parts unknown. That was fine with me. I wanted to be shut of him.

The market went well. I sold out of my clover honey and made a nice wad of cash. I put some bills in my wallet and tucked the rest in my bosom. It was not unheard of that a robber would confront a lone farmer packing up. If that happened to me, the robber would get my wallet with a couple of twenties, but I would have the day's take safely stored on my person. Bess wasn't the only woman to hide money in her bra.

I was a slow packer and was the last of three farmers to break down. I just get slower and slower every year, but I didn't care. It was a beautiful fall day where the air was crisp and the sky a bright cobalt blue—a pleasant time for raking leaves, roasting hot dogs over an open fire, and making caramel apples with the kids.

"Mrs. Reynolds? Josiah?"

I had stored the last box and my chair in the van. "Yeah," I said, turning to Detective Drake. "What do you want now?" I started to have an attitude.

"I am sorry to inform you that Rodney Hiller was found dead yesterday."

At first, I didn't understand what Drake was saying. I made him repeat it. "You found him?" I surmised that Drake had gone to Rod's home to interview him.

"Yes."

As much as I was disappointed in Rod, it was a mighty blow. I sat at the back edge of my van, trying to catch my breath. "What was it—a heart attack? He was having trouble with his heart after his wife died."

Gloating, Drake blurted, "He was murdered!"

"What! How?"

"He was bludgeoned by a hatchet with your fingerprints on it!"

This is really it. I'm going to prison for real, I thought. I held out my wrists for Drake to cuff me and haul my sorry fanny off to jail.

Instead, Drake asked, "Got time for a cup of coffee?"

21

"You seem upset."

My hands clutched a cup of hot tea. "I am. When my husband, Brannon, left me, people took sides. I lost most of my friends, but Rod and Honoria stood by me. They were a great help. I was always grateful to them for that." I peered into my drink, pondering how my friendship with Rod spiraled out of control.

"That's why you looked after him."

"I see you've been talking to people."

Drake nodded.

"I guess you wouldn't be doing your job if you hadn't."

"I thought surely you and Rod had been having an affair."

"Oh, goodness, no. His only love was Honoria. They had a good marriage. They truly delighted in each other's company. Sometimes I was jealous of Honoria. My husband never delighted in my company. I feel ashamed of my petty jealousy now."

"So how did this happen, Mrs. Reynolds?"

"You mean Rod's death?"

"Tell me about your visit with Mr. Hiller."

"I wanted to confront Rod. Nothing about his story made sense. I think it was discovering the gun in Rod's car that made me think he was in collusion with the Statler brothers, but I didn't want to admit it. Then he disappeared from Lady Elsmere's ball. I went upstairs with a tray and he was gone from his room. Where was he?"

"Did he confess to the murder of Skeeter Statler?"

"Rod said he had nothing to do with it. In fact, he was frightened. He thought that the Statler brothers were really trying to kill him out of revenge."

"Honoria was their mother?"

"I think everything that has happened stems from Honoria turning her back on her children."

Drake looked thoughtful. "Why did you pick up the hatchet?"

"I didn't think Rod would hurt me, but you never know what people will do when they are cornered. I thought surely Rod had something to do with Skeeter's death."

"And now?"

"I'm convinced Rod was telling the truth. It was as he said. He was disturbed that the Statler brothers were at Lady Elsmere's ball and sneaked out with the help of his buddy, Saginaw Marshall."

"I talked with Mr. Marshall. It checks out that he and Mr. Hiller left together. The party's security verified they clocked them leaving a little after nine. I don't think Mr. Hiller would have had time to kill Mr. Statler."

I felt relieved to hear Drake clear Rod's name. The truth of the matter was I thought Rod did have time to meet Curry and Skeeter in the corn maze. How else could a fragment of my scarf be in the maze if Rod hadn't gone into it? I kept mum about it. "Speaking of security, have you talked with Manuel? How did he know the Reaper's outfit was on my property?"

"He claims that security cameras picked up a man going on to your property. He wanted to check it out."

"I didn't know that Lady Elsmere had put cameras facing my farm."

"Doesn't your security camera face her property?"

"It faces my hives which back up to Lady Elsmere's place."

Drake smiled. "Splitting hairs, Mrs. Reynolds."

I ignored his comment. "What did Manuel say?"

"He said he had made a call to the police concerning the outfit. I checked with our dispatcher and Manuel did make that call."

"So, he's in the clear?"

"Unless evidence pops up that says different."

I caught a certain tone in Drake's voice. It's sometimes not what people say, but how they say it. "You don't believe him."

"I would say it might be more like someone paid him to retrieve the costume."

"Manuel just received a five thousand dollar bonus from Lady Elsmere."

"That's not very much money anymore. Still, where do I sign up to work for Lady Elsmere? I've never so much as received a Christmas ham from the department."

I began to see Drake in a different light. He worked a high stress job with little financial compensation. His clothes were neat and tidy, but not expensive—possibly from a thrift store. He had nicked himself shaving this morning. There were paint stains on Drake's right hand, so he must have a home. His hair was longish, which meant he didn't have time to see a barber because he was putting in long hours on the job.

"What about the costume?"

"Not a drop of blood on it. To tell you the truth, I think the Grim Reaper was a prank. Had nothing to do with the murder of Skeeter Statler."

"A prank?" It was not the time to dispute Drake's version of events. I had to keep him talking while he was in the mood.

"Any leads on Rod's murder?"

"We are looking for Curry Statler. He had the best motive."

"I think Curry Statler is dead and died the same

night as his brother."

"You don't say why."

"It's a feeling—a hunch."

"There's no evidence to support that theory."

I shrugged. "Where is he then?"

"In hiding." Drake pleaded with me. "If Curry is dead, then who killed Rod Hiller?"

"I don't know. Have you tracked down the camera guy?"

"We don't know who the guy is. We've interviewed Mr. Hiller's friends and no one knew there was an association with the Statler brothers or this camera man."

"What about friends of the Statlers?"

"We've done our job. No one knows anything. What's worse is there is no paper trail."

"What about phone records?"

"We've checked and called every number that looked suspicious. Nothing. The camera guy is a dead end."

"There has got to be a connection."

Drake looked at his watch. "I have to go. Sorry about your friend."

"Thank you."

"If you hear anything, will you let me know?"

"You'll be the first person."

"I know that you have Shaneika Mary Todd on speed dial."

Grinning, I said, "You'll be the second to know."

"That suits me as long as I am in the loop."

"Why the sudden change of heart?"

"What do you mean?"

"Why are you speaking to me like a regular human being rather than a cop?"

"Detective Kelly has known you for a long time."

I said, "Since he was fifteen, but don't hold that against him."

"He offered me some advice."

"Let me guess. You can catch more flies with honey than with vinegar."

"I guess it to be true. You haven't snarled at me once."

"Nor you at me."

"This might be the beginning of a beautiful friendship."

"Let's not get carried away, Detective."

Drake gave me a toothy smile and threw a fiver on the table. Stirring my tea, I watched him leave the diner and drift into the sun-drenched afternoon.

Like I said before, it was a lovely day.

22

I didn't believe for one second that Drake wanted to make peace with me. He was fishing for information. I told him everything I knew. Okay, that's a lie, but almost everything I knew.

After treating myself to an extra piece of pumpkin pie at the diner, I finally got the energy to go home. I was tired and emotionally exhausted from the turmoil of Rod's death. So many questions were unanswered. Pulling into my driveway, I punched in my gate code. Halfway down, I saw Comanche munching grass on the side of the driveway. Oh, dear. How did he get out of his pasture?

I called the Big House and asked Bess if she could send someone to put Comanche back in his field. She replied that she would send a groom over pronto, since she knew I didn't like to deal with male Thoroughbreds, especially this stallion. Comanche was too high-strung, and I had no desire to be bitten or kicked.

Further down the driveway, my llama and her baby

were quietly grazing alongside various sheep, goats, donkeys, and one pig I had taken in. I stopped the van and visited the llama until she threatened to spit on me. Taking the hint, I continued to the Butterfly.

I parked the van and stored items I hadn't sold at the farmers' market. Letting myself in the Butterfly, I was immediately greeted by the aroma of black walnut jam cakes cooling on the kitchen counters. "Hello, Eunice."

Standing at the ovens, Eunice turned around. "How was the market?"

"It's slowing down, but still good. Whatcha doing?"

"I'm making cakes for Thanksgiving and Christmas."

"We have any bookings?"

"We have three Christmas parties so far. I don't want to be rushed this year, so I'm going to get a handle on the cakes and freeze them. There's room in the walk-in freezer. Hope you don't mind."

"Knock yourself out. I'm going to take a shower."

"I'll be a couple hours more."

"No problem. Where's Baby?" I asked, looking around.

She pointed. "He's in the great room with Lincoln."

I nodded and found Lincoln lying on the slate floor coloring. Baby snuggled beside him snoozing. "Hi, Linc."

Lincoln looked up. "Hi, Mrs. Reynolds." He went

back to coloring, not paying any particular attention to me.

"Busy?"

"Un-huh," Lincoln said, pulling out a colored pencil from his pencil box.

"Okay, then." I went into my bedroom and shut the door, chuckling that I had been dismissed by a small boy. Not even Baby raised his head or opened his good eye to greet me. I took a shower, pulled on a thin sweatshirt and matching pants, and did a load of laundry.

When I ventured into the great room, Eunice was finished baking and now cleaning the kitchen. I made myself a sandwich and iced tea before sitting at my Nakashima table. I had to step over Lincoln's art work as pictures were strewn all over the floor.

Eunice called out to Lincoln. "Pick up your drawings, Lincoln, and put away your pencils. We'll be leaving shortly."

Lincoln reluctantly got up and began collecting his pictures until he noticed me eating a sandwich. He wandered over and stood, staring at my sandwich. Baby followed him.

"Want some," I asked, holding out half of my ham sandwich.

He nodded.

"I'll trade you my sandwich for a peek at your drawings."

"Deal."

Lincoln handed me his drawings as I pushed my plate toward him. He climbed on a chair and chomped down on the sandwich. Baby nuzzled him and Lincoln tore the sandwich into quarters, giving my dog his due share.

I studied the drawing, realizing that Lincoln had an artistic flair. There was a nice drawing of Baby, one of my various animals standing around a hay bale, and another of three men standing together in Civil War uniforms in rows of corn, in which a man wore a yellow scarf around his neck.

"Linc."

"Yeah?"

"Is this in the corn maze from the party?" I asked, sliding the drawing over to him.

"Yeah," he said, between bites.

"Did you hear what the men were discussing?"

"Yep."

"What did the men talk about?"

"They were fussing with each other about a gun."

"Can you remember what they said specifically?"

"Naw, they ran when the monster jumped out at them. So I ran, too."

"Is that when you bumped into me?"

"Yeah."

"Is that the monster dressed in a brown robe and carrying a scythe?"

"Is a scythe a big sword?"

"Sort of."

"Yep."

"You say 'yes ma'am' to Mrs. Reynolds," Eunice said, standing behind Lincoln and staring at the drawing.

I asked, "Did the men run together?"

"Naw, I mean, no ma'am. Everyone split up and ran down different paths."

"Did you see one of the men get hurt?"

"One man tripped and fell."

"I thought you ran when they started running?"

"Not then. It was so fast. I didn't see the monster at first. They ran, the man fell, and the monster stood over him. Then I ran as well."

"No one pushed the man down?"

"No, ma'am. He was running and fell."

"Did the man get back up?"

"I don't know. I was running."

"Why do you think the men ran? There were three of them and one of the Grim Reaper?"

"Because he was scary."

"Could you recognize the three men if you saw them again?"

"Yes, ma'am."

"Just a moment." I went for my purse hanging on the coat rack in the hallway, retrieving my phone. I clicked on PHOTOS and handed the phone to Lincoln. "Go through these and see if you recognize anyone."

"Okay."

Lincoln thumbed through my photos carefully between sips of my drink as well. Finally, he said, "This man. He was one of the three men."

I looked at the image. It was one taken of Rod and me at the Civil War practice session. We were both smiling, looking genuinely happy.

This was more proof that Rod had lied to me about being in the corn maze.

What else had he lied to me about?

23

What was Detective Drake really investigating—a murder, an attempted murder, fraud, theft? Was he trying to put the pieces of a puzzle into some coherent fashion as I was doing?

Thinking about my conversation with Drake during the rest of the evening, I finally made a decision. It was not the prudent thing to do nor the safe thing to do, but it was the right thing to do. Since Honoria's death, Rod had given me a key to his home in case of emergencies.

On All Hallow's Eve, after retrieving Rod's key, I called for Baby, who was taking a nap in his doggy bed located in the great room. Off we went to Rod's house for a snooping expedition. I did not approve of Rod's shenanigans, but he was my friend—still.

I felt better about Rod, now there was a witness who could testify that Skeeter fell by accident inside the maze. Perhaps Skeeter fell upon a rock. There was still the probability that someone bashed in his skull after

172

he fell, but I was beginning to think this was not the case. It was looking more like a simple mishap.

Getting closer to Rod's house, I kept my eyes open, looking warily for police cars. I did not want to be caught entering his home. If I had a smacking of a police stakeout, I would turn about and head for the hills, so to speak.

No cars in sight, I slowly drove down the road to Rod's house, which sat near the stream of his favorite agate haunt and parked my car behind the barn.

The tan framed house looked sad. The grass needed mowing and weeds had shot up in the garden. It looked like Rod had given up on the place. The trees were really shedding now, causing my feet to crunch on dry leaves littering the pathway to the back door. I picked up scattered newspapers strewn on the lawn and gathered Rod's mail collecting in his mailbox.

I stole a look at Baby. He was busy sniffing and since he was showing no signs of alarm, I let myself in via the back door. Baby followed.

The house already smelled musty. I flipped on the light switch. Good, the power was still on. There was a clutter of mail already on the kitchen table. I threw the newest letters on the pile.

Making myself a cup of tea, I sat at the table going through the mail. I separated the mail into bundles— bills and junk mail. Since Rod had neither kith nor kin, who was going to take care of these bills, his property, and the funeral arrangements?

I needed to find Rod's will. I looked for an address book. I couldn't find one. Does anyone keep an old fashioned address book anymore besides me? Apparently not Honoria or Rod. The police must have Rod's phone, so that was a dead end. I went through drawers and nightstands, looking for safe deposit box keys or business cards from a lawyer—anything to help me put Rod's affairs in order. I didn't find anything. The police must have swept through with a fine tooth comb.

I knew Rod kept important items in his work shed, so Baby and I walked the dusty path to the shed. Since the lock for the shed had been busted, I knew the police had searched through it. I wondered if they knew Rod kept his best agate under the floorboards in a special hidey hole. I turned on the light and faced a cluttered, grimy work area. Everywhere was agate—raw agate and then polished agate cabochons for jewelers. On a work bench I found a slew of orders for agate. I wondered if the jewelers had been notified of Rod's death while I continued to look for documents. Isn't it funny that each human being is defined by paper—a birth certificate, a marriage license, a passport, a house deed, and finally a will.

A board squeaked as I walked over it. I pressed on it again. It felt loose. Grabbing a chair and a screw driver, I knelt down and pried up the board, which came up easily. Peering inside, I discovered a gray metal box with a handle on top. Using the chair and Baby as leverage, I got back up. I can get down, but getting off my knees is always a problem if I don't have something to pull myself up. The box was stubborn to pry open, but with the help of the rusty screwdriver, I finally yanked it open. Inside was a bundle of papers, including love letters from Rod to Honoria dating back twenty years. I stored the letters in my purse with the intent of putting them into Rod's casket. No one needed to read them. Certainly not the police.

I pulled out other important looking documents, carrying them to the window for better light. I had gone through most of them when I heard a motorcycle. I looked out the window.

It was Curry Statler!

24

So Curry wasn't dead, after all! Wonders never cease.

That put him right at the top of my list for killing Rod.

My heart started beating loudly and I felt faint. My car was on the other side of the house. How could I get to it without Curry seeing me?

In a situation like this, bravado is always the best defense. Pulling the stun gun from my pocket, I walked outside the work shed and stood in the yard. "CURRY STATLER! I want to talk with you."

Curry lumbered out from the house, slamming the back door. "Who are you, lady?"

"My name is Josiah Reynolds, and I just notified the police that you are here. They've been looking for you. They want to talk to you concerning the death of your brother."

A pained look flashed across Curry's face. "I came to have it out with Rod once and for all. Where is he? In the shed?"

Unless Curry had gone to the Royal Academy of Dramatic Art, I doubt he could fake his way out of a paper bag. "Where you've been, young man?"

"Hiding out in the mountains with my grandparents. I came to talk with the police, but I wanted to confront Rod first."

"You have an appointment with the police?"

"Yeah. A Detective Drake."

"Why do you want to see Rod?"

"I want to know what happened in the corn maze. Did he kill my brother?"

"And if Rod says no, then what?"

Curry ignored me. "ROD! ROD! COME OUT, YOU COWARD! FACE ME LIKE A MAN!"

"Curry, Rod can't answer you."

Shooting me a hateful look, Curry asked, "Why not?"

"Because he's dead, son."

25

I made us both a cup of tea, not that Curry was a tea drinker, but the act of making tea and sipping it calms the nerves. Curry picked up his tea mug with a large, fleshy hand and sniffed.

"You can sweeten it, if you like," I suggested, indicating the sugar bowl.

Curry's hands shook as he tried to tear open a yellow packet of artificial sugar and dump it in the mug. He didn't look so big and tough as he struggled. I tore a packet open and handed it to him.

"Thank you kindly."

I nodded while observing him. Curry had shaved his straggly beard and given himself a flat top, which enhanced his wide fleshy cheek bones. He was a big man with a wide chest and hips to match. There were no six pack abs on that body, but Curry was strong. Very strong. Usually, big men like Curry had a mild disposition, but I didn't feel that with him. Yet I didn't feel afraid. It was because of Baby.

Baby didn't respond to him fearfully. He went over to Curry and placed his head on the man's lap, wanting to be petted. Curry obliged him and stroked my dog's head much of the time we talked. I trust my dog's instincts. If Baby's not afraid, then I'm not either.

I handed Curry a spoon.

"Thanks."

"Want to tell me about your deal with Rod?"

Curry shook his head.

"Consider it a practice run with the police."

"I wanted to talk with them before they came huntin' for me."

"Will you have a lawyer with you?"

"Yes."

"That's good." I hesitated for a moment. We both sat in silence until I said, "I'm waiting."

Curry took a deep breath. "Rod contacted us about making some good money. He had seen our videos and said we were going about it all wrong. Skeeter and I didn't care about rocks. We just wanted to do something fun—make a name for ourselves. Others were doing it on social media. Why not us? We had nothing else going on for us, so Skeeter and me decided to take the chance. When Rod called, we listened to his pitch and said yes."

"I thought the two of you hated Rod."

"I was too little to remember when Mama and Dad got divorced. I don't know why Dad got sole custody of us. He was a holy mess. We spent most of our childhood with our daddy's grandparents."

"Did Honoria keep in touch?"

"We didn't think so. When Mama passed away, Rod gave us letters and cards she had sent, but were returned by our grandparents. My grandparents were old-school. They thought Mama was a Jezebel." Curry took a sip of tea and then another. "We found out later Mama paid child support for both of us until we were eighteen."

"How did that make you feel?"

"Confused. We visited Mama a few times, but it felt uncomfortable. We were embarrassed at how our kinfolk treated her, and she was embarrassed that she didn't fight for custody. It was a stalemate."

"Why didn't you know that Rod had died?"

"Like I said, my grandparents are old-school—no computers, no papers, no smart phones. When they want to know something, they go into town."

"What about *your* phone?"

Curry painfully grinned. "No service either."

"What did you know about Skeeter?"

"I heard from a friend that Skeeter had died from a blow to the head in the corn maze. I came into town to make funeral arrangements. I'm taking Skeeter back up to the hills to be buried alongside Dad."

"What did you think when Skeeter didn't come out of the corn maze?"

"We had parked off the road and climbed over the fence. After getting out of the maze, I ran to the car and waited for Skeeter, but he didn't come. When I heard the sirens, I boogied out, thinking we would catch up later."

"Why did you think the police were coming?"

"To arrest us on suspicion of attempted murder. You know—at the Civil War reenactment. All we wanted to do was talk to Rod, but he wouldn't answer our phone calls. That's why we showed up."

"Can you tell me what that was about?"

"We wanted to confront Rod on why he switched the ammo in the gun."

"Tell me about this entire scam the three of you were doing."

Curry looked offended. "It wasn't a scam. We were trying to get noticed. All those reality shows are scripted. That's all we were doing."

"What went wrong?" I asked, pouring myself more tea from the kettle before turning off the stove.

"We were contacted by an agent who said to send him something special, so Rod thought up a final altercation at the reenactment. It was to be spectacular with the battle—all that pomp and clamor."

"Why use a modern .22 instead of a period pistol?"

"They are very unreliable. Rod only had one, so he gave that one to Skeeter and the .22 to me. A modern firearm would look fierce. Like we meant business."

"Why did you load real ammo in the .22?" I knew Curry would deny this, but I wanted to hear what he would say.

"We didn't. We were as surprised as Rod when he got hit. I fired the gun. He fell like he was supposed to and then we blended back in with our compatriots. That was the plan. It wasn't until the siren sounded that we knew something went wrong."

"And you still put the gun in Rod's glove compartment?"

"We followed the plan. We didn't know that Rod had been hurt until we saw the ambulance going across the field. I can tell you that Skeeter and me were relieved when Rod called and told us to meet him at the party."

"I though you said Rod wouldn't return your phone calls."

"I said he wouldn't *answer* our phone calls, but he finally called us, asking us to come to the ball. We had invitations as we really signed up to be reenactors. We were legit in that."

"If you parked your car off the road and climbed over the fence, the police will take this as an admission that Rod didn't know you were coming. I don't still understand why you parked off the side of the road."

"Because old lady Elmere's place has too many gates and guards. We wanted to put our car where we could reach it in a hurry. All we had to do was jump over a fence to get to it." Curry paused and chewed on a thumb nail, remembering.

"Go on."

"We didn't know what Rod had planned. Was the shooting of live ammo an accident or did Rod set us up? We made that scene in the Big House as protection. You know—so people would notice us."

"That they did, indeed."

"It was dumb, I agree. Those reenactor boys take those uniforms seriously, but I don't know why they got on us so. Rod was wearing a general's uniform and he wasn't entitled."

"Lady Elsmere asked Rod to wear that Confederate uniform to escort her down the staircase—sorta like a Grant and Lee on either side of her."

"Oh." Curry rubbed the day old stubble on his chin.

"Let's get back to the shooting. It was a miracle the bullet didn't glance off Rod and strike another soldier. You guys were stupid."

"I swear I didn't switch the ammo in the gun. I swear on the Bible."

"Then who did?"

"Skeeter and I thought Rod had."

"Curry, use your brain and what little sense you have. Why would Rod put live ammo in a gun that was to be pointed and fired at him?"

"That's what Rod said in his defense. We met at the back of the corn maze where we thought no one could hear us and had it out."

"What was the conclusion?"

"There wasn't one. Some idiot in a monk's costume with a huge blade jumped out at us, and we took off."

"Going down the same pathways?"

"No, we scattered in different directions. I think Rod went through the corn. The corn rows were wider apart in the back."

"Why run?"

"Duh. We didn't want the monk to see our faces in case he overheard."

I asked, "Any idea of who it was?"

"Nope. Now it's my turn to ask some questions."

"Go right ahead."

"If Rod didn't kill my brother, then who?"

"I don't think anyone killed your brother. I think he slipped and fell on a rock."

Curry looked sad when he asked, "Then why are the police making such a big deal?"

I gave an over-innocent shrug. "They are investigating a *possible* murder. It's what they do."

"How did Rod die?"

"He was killed with his own hatchet."

"Wheee. That's cold." He shoved the mug away. "You still think I killed Rod?"

"I don't know, but I do have a motive."

"What's that?"

I held up Rod's will. "Honoria and Rod left this

place to you and Skeeter. It's all yours now. Quite a coincidence, Curry."

Curry flinched and clucked with his teeth, saying, "Ain't it though."

26

The police had no evidence against Curry for the murder of Rod Hiller. He had an airtight alibi for the time of Rod's death. He was in the mountains as he claimed. After the cops cut him loose, Curry Statler had no legal impairment to stop him from claiming Rod's place, his savings, and all of the agate.

I will say that Curry did right by Rod. He claimed the body and held a funeral, even though it was a closed casket due to Rod's injuries. Before the service, I snuck in early, opened the casket, and placed his love letters to Honoria under his suit jacket near his heart. "Good bye, old friend," I said, thinking about his abiding love for his wife and trying not to stare at Rod's gauze-wrapped face. "I wish your last days had been more peaceful, but you're with Honoria now. You both take care of each other."

I gently closed the casket and sat in the back waiting for the service. People trickled in a few at a time until the room was filled with friends and associates. I must say all of Rod's buddies gave him a rousing send-off, telling wild stories of his misspent youth and sobering passions later on in life. An hour went by quickly until the minister asked us to stand for a last prayer. As soon as we murmured *amen,* instructions to follow the hearse to the graveyard were piped in over a loudspeaker system. I followed the others to our cars and got in the queue for the graveyard. I turned on my windshield wipers as it had started spitting rain.

At the gravesite, Rod's Civil War buddies, dressed in Civil War attire, fired a three-volley salute in his honor with Saginaw acting as the commanding officer. In fact, he had taken Rod's former position in the company.

Sadly, I watched them lower Rod's casket next to Honoria. As soon as the casket hit the bottom of the grave, Curry strolled off, while many of the farmers, the agate hounds, and the Civil War reenactors lingered to wonder out loud about the manner of Rod's death and who murdered him. It was then I spied a young man taking pictures from behind a tree.

Walking as though I was going to my car, I doubled back, catching the young man unawares. Grabbing his digital camera, I asked, "Who the hell are you?"

Startled, the man lunged at me. "Give me back my camera. You have no right."

"I'm gonna take this camera and bust you upside the head if you don't tell me what I want to know."

One of the farmers yelled, "You need help, Josiah?"

"Yeah, bring some boys over here."

The farmer motioned and Irene Meckler with her husband, Jefferson Davis Meckler walked over.

"What's happening?" Irene Meckler asked. She and her husband sold flowers at the farmers' market. Rod had his booth between both of ours.

I handed Jefferson the camera. "He was taking pictures of the funeral."

He flipped through the pictures. "Sure enough." He handed the camera to Irene.

"There's no crime in taking pictures of a funeral," the man said, pushing back strands of hair which had escaped his pony tail. "Be careful. You'll get my camera wet from the rain. It's an expensive piece of equipment."

"You know many murderers insert themselves into the investigation. If you were on the level, you would have been out in the open filming like that cop over there." I pointed to Officer Snow filming cars' license plate numbers and who got in which car.

"I'm . . . I'm no murderer. I swear." He grabbed for his camera, but Irene held it out of his reach.

"Who are you then?" I asked, beckoning to Officer Snow.

The man pulled out a wallet and flipped it open, showing us his driver's license. "My name is Noble Spradlin."

Snow came over. "What's the problem?"

Irene handed Officer Snow the camera. "This guy was filming the funeral."

Spradlin thrust his wallet at Snow. "My name is Noble Spradlin."

Officer Snow said, "Take your license out of your wallet, sir."

"I'm not doing any harm!" protested Spradlin.

"Then you won't mind me checking you in the computer system." Snow cradled the camera as he headed for his vehicle. The rest of us surrounded Spradlin so he couldn't escape. As sweat dripped off his temple, he used his thumb to wipe it off.

"It's an awfully cool day to be sweating, Spradlin," I commented.

"You have no right to look at my camera. I'm going to sue you all."

"Just be quiet," Jefferson warned, wiping away some drizzle from his face.

Several minutes later, Snow came back and handed the camera to Spradlin. "He's clean."

"I have a few questions," I said, irritated that Snow was going to let Spradlin go.

"Have at it," Snow said, walking away.

I turned to the young man still pinned against the tree. "Why?"

"Because I was paid to do so."

"Who paid you?"

"Curry Statler. I'm making a tape for him to send to

Hollywood—*Tribulations of a Kentucky Rock Hound."*

Irene snapped her fingers, saying, "I remember you now. You were at the farmers' market when the Statler brothers and Rod got into a row."

Spradlin grinned. "Some of my best work."

"You are the elusive camera man," I said.

"I've filmed everything they ever did. With all the footage I've got, I can put together a little reality show about rock hunting or a documentary about Rod's murder."

"Confirm something for me. Was the feud between Rod and the Statler brothers staged or real?"

"Totally staged. Totally."

"What happens now that Rod and Skeeter are deceased?" Irene asked.

"Curry will soldier on. The offer for a show is still on the table. In fact, these deaths make great drama for the tape."

I asked, "What's in it for you?"

"I follow on Curry's coattails to Tinsel Town."

Our faces must have shown our disgust because Spradlin sputtered, "Hey look. I didn't hurt anyone."

"Seems to me like you have a motive," I said.

"I heard how Rod died—how he was bludgeoned with a hatchet. Too messy for me. If I were going to kill someone, I'd shoot them. I wouldn't have the stomach for anything else. If you're looking for Rod's murderer, look closer to home." He nodded toward the

Civil War reenactors.

"Were you present at the Remembrance Ball?"

"I heard about the Grim Reaper. That wasn't me."

"You didn't answer the lady's question," Jefferson said.

"Curry and Skeeter were scared. They thought Rod had set them up and were going to have it out with him."

I sighed. Here we go again with the stupid theory that Rod put live ammo in his own gun. "Why would Rod have live ammo in a gun that was to be pointed at him?"

"Maybe he wanted to commit suicide? Who knows why people do crazy stuff?"

"Do you really think that?"

"Not really. It's what Curry and Skeeter thought. I told them the screw-up didn't come from Rod."

"Why do you suggest the Civil War actors had something to do with Rod's demise?"

"I spent two days filming there and overheard a lot of bickering and complaining amongst the soldiers. They are not the tight-knit brotherhood you think they are. If I were to pinpoint a motive for Rod's death, I would say—envy."

I glanced over at the group of reenactors still hanging about, gossiping.

"Thank you. Sorry we frightened you." I said, still staring at the Civil War buffs.

"No problem," Spradlin said. "I've been recording this entire interaction. Will make a great intro." He pointed to a flag pin attached to his coat lapel. "Newest thing on the market. See ya suckers later." Spradlin pushed through us, laughing.

"Well, don't that beat all," Irene said, staring after Spradlin.

Her husband, Jefferson said, "We're going to look like a bunch of redneck vigilantes."

"Excuse me," I said after seeing Shooby leave the group of Civil War enthusiasts and head for his car. I hurried over. "Mr. Shooby. Mr. Shooby. May I speak with you, sir?"

Shooby turned around. He was a handsome man in his United States Colored Troop uniform, standing over six feet. He had a warm-hued complexion, hazel-green expressive eyes, and close cropped dark hair. "Yes?"

"My name is Josiah Reynolds. I was a friend of Rod's."

"I remember you talking with him on the day of the practice."

"You remember me out of all those people?"

Shooby gave a gentle smile—almost beatific. "Not many women have your hair color. You stand out in a crowd, Mrs. Reynolds."

I blushed. I didn't know if Shooby was complimenting me or not. I wish I could say my hair color was natural, but since my accident my real color has been gristle gray. Gray doesn't go well with my green eyes, so I dye my hair. It is pretty close to my natural red before the accident. Like I said before—I come from Viking stock. "Rod thought highly of you."

"That's nice to hear."

"Do you know if any of the Civil War buffs had a beef with Rod?"

"Why do you ask?"

"I heard a rumor there was complaining among the reenactors. Did any of the complaints have to do with him?"

"When you get a group of people together, there are always a couple of whiners and naysayers. It's human nature."

"Anyone in particular?"

"I'm not saying. I will not spur negative connotations upon my Civil War brethren." Shooby straightened the brim of his hat. "I've read about you. You're supposed to be a sleuth of some sort—so sleuth."

"Mr. Shooby, there's no need to be snippy. I'm just trying to discover who murdered my friend."

"And you're not listening, my good woman. I'm not saying the rumors are false. I'm saying I will not comment. You are a woman of intelligence, so you know to investigate those closest to Rod and work your way out from there." Shooby tipped his hat. "Good day to you, ma'am."

Well, if that don't beat all!

27

Lady Elsmere opened her home for a gathering after the funeral. All of Rod's friends were invited. Since there was free food and an open bar, many of the people at the funeral showed up. I thought this was an excellent opportunity to do as Mr. Shooby suggested—sleuth.

Since the reenactors were tight lipped about each other, I sought out the man with the nagging wife, whom Rod had pointed out at the skirmish practice. Once I had spotted him, I searched for his wife. I saw a plump woman wearing an obvious blonde wig, hand the man a plate of food before sitting beside him looking bored. That must be the wife.

I fixed myself a plate of beaten biscuits with ham and tiny roast beef sandwiches and stood in a corner waiting for an opportunity to talk with her. It wasn't long before her husband finished his plate and wandered off to join his compatriots gathered around the bar.

The man's wife watched him leave with contempt.

This was my chance. I moseyed over and said, "Is this seat free?"

"Help yourself," she said, still eyeing her husband yuck it up with the boys.

"My name is Josiah." I held out my hand.

She stared at my hand for a second and then shook it. "My name is Miriam."

"Nice to meet you."

"Are you a friend of Rod's?"

"I'm sorry to say I never met him, but my husband was a buddy."

"I'm the same," I lied. "Isn't it awful about the rivalry in the ranks? All that anger over a game."

Miriam leaned toward me and whispered. "These men take this too seriously. The money my husband has spent on uniforms and equipment makes me furious. I've had to do without because of his hobby."

"Me, too." I let Miriam vent until she ran out of steam. It was then I whispered conspiratorially, "I heard someone had a problem with Rod. Who do you think that might be?"

"I don't think. I know. My husband told me all about it."

"Do tell."

Miriam glanced about to see if anyone was listening. "Maybe I shouldn't say."

"Noted," I said, before biting into a ham biscuit.

"Wouldn't want you to betray a confidence."

Miriam scoffed. "As if I care. Come closer."

I scooted my chair next to hers. "Go on."

"See that man over there in the Union captain uniform?"

I nodded.

"That's Saginaw Marshall. He and Rod got into it a few years ago when Rod made the rank of captain. Saginaw recruited Rod and felt slighted when Rod became an officer before he did."

"I thought that all the actors had to take a test to advance."

"That's just it. Saginaw scored higher on his test, but the command was given to Rod."

"Why?"

"Saginaw had a bad disposition, and it was felt he lacked leadership abilities."

"They must have made up because he and Rod were the best of friends."

"Were they?" Miriam arched her eyebrows. "Were they?"

"Rod liked Saginaw."

"And now Rod Hiller is dead. I'm just saying."

"How long ago was this?"

"Six years, maybe. Rod had to drop out awhile when his wife took sick. Saginaw took over command until Rod came back and took up his post again. My husband was surprised when Rod ran around with

Saginaw when he returned."

"The skirmish was Rod's last hurrah. He said he was getting too old."

"The question to ask is if Saginaw knew it was Rod's last hurrah. Makes you think, doesn't it?"

"Yes, it does."

Taking a last gulp of whiskey, Miriam's husband beckoned to her.

"My lord and master is calling me. He wants to leave." Miriam stood and laid her messy plate on the chair. "Nice to have met you, Josiah. Hope I didn't speak out of turn."

"It was nice meeting you, too. Take care."

I watched Saginaw laugh it up with the boys. He did seem overly cheery and boisterous. Perhaps it was time to put a little rat poison in his drink.

Figuratively, I mean.

28

I sauntered over to the bar and ordered a bourbon neat.

Saginaw, half-sheets to the wind, slapped me on the back. "Hey, Josiah. Wasn't that a grand send-off for our buddy, Rod?"

I swirled around and whispered close to his ear. "I know Rod's murderer enjoyed it." I looked Saginaw straight in the eye.

Saginaw stumbled backward, looking stunned. "What did you say?"

"You heard me. I know all about it. At the first chance, I'm gonna tell the police." I picked up my drink and made my way outside to the corn maze. Seeing Saginaw peer at me through the window, I proceeded into the maze.

I meandered through the maze until I came to a bench. I sat and waited.

It wasn't too long until Saginaw found me.

"Hello, Saginaw. I knew you'd follow."

"What do you know?"

"It could only be you. Once I discovered you resented Rod for making rank before you, the pieces fell into place."

"That was a long time ago. We moved on."

"Rod did for sure. He never understood your deep animosity—that is until Rod claimed his post again. Oh, the resentment you must have felt. Since you played your part of a good friend, Rod must have confided in you about the scheme he and the Statler brothers were playing. You put live ammo in the gun he hid in his tent. It was the only place the gun could have been during Friday's practice. I checked Rod's truck on Friday and the gun was not in the glove compartment."

"Curry has admitted that he placed the .22 in Rod's truck."

"But he didn't have the gun until it was given to him on Friday. I suppose that the transfer of the .22 gun into Curry's possession was to take place during the altercation between the Statlers and Rod in front of his tent, but there were too many witnesses. Even you started filming with your phone."

"No gun exchanged hands during that argument. You can see for yourself on the video."

"I know, so Rod asked you to take the .22 and the one shot pistol to the brothers to avoid suspicion. You agreed, believing it to be your chance of switching the blanks for real ammo."

"If that were true, why doesn't Curry tell the police?"

"I think you laid the guns in the Statler tent without either of the brothers seeing you. They probably thought it was Rod who laid the guns there."

"I loved Rod like a brother."

"You may have loved him, but you resented him as well. He made rank over you, and you could not let that go. It just ate at you over the years."

"I felt sorry for Rod. He lost Honoria and became a man waiting to die."

"That is until he came up with this scheme with the Statler brothers, and it was working too. They were getting nibbles from reality programming producers. That was the end-all for you. Rod was coming out on top again. Your envy just ate at your innards. It was like a cancer."

"You talk like a crazy woman."

As soon as the name calling started, I knew I was on the right track. "You would never be suspected because the Statler brothers would take the rap. Only the plan didn't work. Either the gun misfired or Curry is such a lousy shot, Rod was only wounded."

"Can't prove a thing. Supposition, that's all this is."

"Then you came up with another plan. Rod had been grazed by a bullet and was weak—not thinking straight. Again, he must have confided to you that the

Statler brothers wanted to meet with him. You suggested they meet in the maze. He agreed, so you put another plan into motion."

Saginaw stepped closer. "You look very vulnerable sitting on that cold bench. I'm a head taller and have fifty pounds on you. I could wring your neck very easily."

I continued talking while tightening my hand around my stun gun. "You were the Grim Reaper. I really thought it was Curry at first. The outfit and the entrance to the ball was dramatic, just Curry's style. He has a bold personality. Likes attention."

"Maybe I wore another costume, so what? It was a costume party."

"It was another attempt to kill Rod. You'd hoped to find Rod alone in the maze and kill him with the scythe, but you didn't reach him first. The Statlers did. The three of them scattered when they saw you, and Skeeter had the misfortune of falling and hitting his head on a rock."

Saginaw grinned. "You sure about that?"

The blood in my veins froze. "I'm not sure what you mean. Skeeter didn't fall onto a rock?"

Saginaw gave a mean grin. "You can blab all you want. Go ahead. There is no evidence."

"I think there is a tracking device somewhere with your fingerprints on it—probably in your car. Then there is the Reaper outfit you stashed on my farm.

What you didn't know is that I have deer cams all across my farm. I got a good shot of you stashing the costume on my farm."

Saginaw's eyes widened.

"You didn't know the police discovered it. I'm sure they have finished their saliva and DNA testing on the mask. Now with the deer cam footage, I'd say they have a lot of questions for you."

"You're full of it."

"When the plan for the reenactment didn't work, you took the direct method. You went to Rod's house and as you were walking up to him, picked up the hatchet and hit him with it. Rod didn't see it coming—not from his good friend."

Saginaw's face contorted into a hideous mask of rage and hate. His mouth tightened into a small hole from which he spewed his loathing. "Rod didn't deserve his promotion. He stole respect from me." Saginaw bitterly laughed. "I brought Rod into the organization only to have him supplant me. That's not fair."

"It's only a matter of time before the police come for you, Saginaw. You'd better run."

Saginaw moved toward me.

I held up my stun gun. "Run, Saginaw, run!"

The man uttered a frightened moan and quickly turned, running out of the maze.

Taking a deep breath, I asked, "Did you get all that?"

Noble Spradlin emerged from the corn stalks, taking out his earbuds. "Recorded it all. Video and audio. Saginaw is gonna fry."

"I guess this will make you a big man in Hollywood with a confession to Rod's murder."

Spradlin winked. "Keep your fingers crossed, baby."

"You better find a policeman. There are several here. I think Detective Drake will be very interested to see your video."

"I'd better make a copy before Drake sees it. He might want to confiscate it. Thanks, Mrs. Reynolds. You did me a high-five. I'm sure to get a one-way ticket to Hollywood now."

I didn't reply. Spradlin melted into the corn stalks again to hide as he wasn't sure Saginaw had found his way out of the maze. I felt Saginaw had. I didn't feel his negative energy any longer, but still I waited.

After twenty long minutes, I heard my name angrily called. It was Drake. There was no doubt there was to be another lecture, another threat of arrest, and another media story connecting my name to murder.

What can I say in my defense?

I'm good at solving puzzles—or mazes as it were.

EPILOGUE

"You wanted to see me?" I asked, sticking my head into Lady Elsmere's bedroom.

Looking regal as ever in a royal blue silk wrapper, June folded her newspaper. "You made the papers again."

"I know."

"I see Saginaw Marshall was arrested for the murder of Rod, but not for Skeeter Statler."

"Skeeter's cause of death was deemed inconclusive. He may have fallen when fleeing the Grim Reaper."

"Wouldn't that be a manslaughter charge then?"

"No one witnessed Skeeter fall, but Lincoln, and I'm not going to tell the police about that. The boy's gone through enough. Scared out of his wits."

"If you say so. Was Lincoln ever interviewed by the police?"

"No, but the DA thinks convicting Saginaw for the murder of Rod will be enough to put him behind bars for a long time. That's all that matters—to me anyway."

June patted the folded newspaper with her index finger. "There are several titles for you now. Kentucky's Mistress of Mayhem, the Queen Bee of Murder, and my favorite, the Countess of Chaos. Detective Drake is quoted as saying, 'Where you go, people drop dead.'"

"Kind of unfair for Drake to say that. I mean I didn't kill these people."

"You do have the unpleasant habit of stumbling over corpses. People are asking me if you are going to be present when invited to my affairs. You have everyone scared to death of you."

"I don't know what to say, June. I'm very sorry."

"Don't be. My invitations now have a ninety-nine percent acceptance rate. Everyone wants to come and see who drops dead at my next fête."

"Your friends are horrible," I said, laughing. I shouldn't have laughed. Murder is not something to sneer about, but still I laughed. How else could I respond?

"Yes, aren't they," June said, "but most people are horrible. It's a fact of life. We live amongst monsters."

"That's a cheery thought."

"Speaking of cheery thoughts, this might tickle your toes." June reached under her pillow and brought out a wrinkled, folded business envelope. "I meant to give this to you weeks ago, but events got in the way. I wanted to wait until things had calmed down before I gave it to you." She handed me the sealed envelope.

"What is it?"

"Just open it, Josiah."

I looked curiously at the envelope and gingerly tore it open.

"This is between you and me," June said, seriously. "No one else. Keep it quiet."

I pulled out a cashier's check for two million dollars.

"Of course, the government will want to take half of that. Matt has come up with a plan for you to keep most of it. He's a good tax attorney."

Stunned, I asked, "What am I to do with it?"

"Buy more bees. Do good works. Plan for the day your kidneys go south on you permanently."

"How do you know about my kidneys?"

"I know everything, Josiah. Everything. Even what happened at Cumberland Falls." June gave me a *knowing* glare.

I froze. Unwelcome thoughts came swirling in my head. How did June know about my kidney issue? What else did she have knowledge of? Did she know about Detective Goetz killing Fred O'Nan for me? And why give me this money now?

You know what I did?

I took the check and laid it on my bedroom dresser under an empty perfume bottle. June and I never spoke of it again.

It is still there—waiting to be cashed.

Just waiting. Waiting. Waiting.

Books By Abigail Keam

Josiah Reynolds Mysteries

Mona Moon Mysteries

About The Author

Hi, I'm Abigail Keam. I write the award-winning *Josiah Reynolds Mystery Series* and the *1930s Mona Moon Mystery Series*. In addition, I write *The Princess Maura Tales* (Epic Fantasy) and the *Last Chance For Love Series* (Sweet Romance).

I am a professional beekeeper and have won awards for my honey from the Kentucky State Fair. I live in a metal house with my husband and various critters on a cliff overlooking the Kentucky River. I would love to hear from you, so please contact me.

Until we meet again, dear friend, happy reading!